SHADOW EMPRESS

C.N. CRAWFORD

COREY PRESS INC

CHAPTER 1

ALI

I crouched at the forest's edge, my attention focused outward, away from the reassuring darkness. I was scanning Vanaheim's great plains, looking for the return of my men in my new kingdom. I'd sent three out on a scouting party to the west. Now, as the shadows grew longer and the sky tinged with red, my stomach clenched. Something had gone wrong.

Swegde, the former Regent of the Vanir, crouched next to me. He wore buckskin trousers and a black vest that exposed thick, muscular forearms. His dark hair draped over enormous shoulders. Of course, he was armed to the teeth. A short sword on one hip, a hunting knife strapped to the other, and slung over his back a bow and quiver full of arrows. He was ready for anything—and anything could happen.

"Where are they?" I asked. "They said noon, it's nearly sundown. They should be back by now."

He glanced at me for just a second. "Don't worry about them. Worry about your knife-throwing skills. Practice in your mind."

I sighed. "We've been practicing nonstop, Swegde. I think I'm good."

"We will be moving on to bear wrestling soon. As Empress of the Vanaheim, you must be skilled at bear wrestling. Focus on that."

My forehead wrinkled. "But—why?"

"It's a Vanir custom. We've been over this. You killed the Emperor, now you must fill his role. Wrestling bears is part of that. Don't question it."

I leaned against an oak trunk. Usually, I *liked* it here in the shadows. The forest reminded me of the Shadow Caverns, the caves where I'd spent my childhood. The massive oaks formed a canopy so thick it nearly blocked out the sun, and the air hung still and heavy with the scent of ferns.

I walked every day among the ancient trees—collecting the little golden chanterelles that grew on rotting stumps, listening to the sounds of tiny animals scurrying unseen in the gloom. I searched the dark places for pixies and fairies.

Here, I felt at home. Almost at ease.

Almost, but not quite.

Because always, I carried a sharp gnawing emptiness—the hole that Galin had left when he disappeared.

I pushed the memory of him deep under the surface, trying not to let myself feel that pain. It was a pain that shouldn't exist, anyway. I'd severed our mating bond. There was no reason for me to feel anything at all.

Swegde had drilled into my head that as Empress, you had to separate your emotions from the business of ruling. He wasn't wrong about that. What good would it do to pine over someone? None at all.

Beyond the trees, wind rippled the tall grasses like waves on an ocean. Birds flew in and out of the blowing fronds, collecting stems and leaves to build their nests. Great herds of bison and horses grazed in the distance. While I loved the dark comfort of the forest, the Vanir loved the grasslands. The fields provided food for our herds of cattle and horses, a place to run and ride.

But when I walked in them, I only felt exposed, like some massive eagle might swoop down at any moment and carry me away. Even now I could see a kettle of vultures circling in the late afternoon sun. Creepy as Hel.

They were growing more numerous, revolving in an ever-widening gyre of black wings.

"Those are vultures, right?" I said. "Do you think there's something dead out there?"

Swegde nodded. "One of the horses, most likely. They break their legs in prairie dog holes."

I stared at the vultures as they glided in great circles, round and round, their movements almost hypnotic. More of them now than even a few seconds ago.

"Are there usually this many?"

"No—" Swegde began, but I held up a finger, cutting him off. I'd heard a noise.

"Did you hear that?"

"What?" he whispered.

I heard it again. The sky was blue as a robin's egg, but it sounded like thunder.

Swegde frowned, even as I squinted, staring across the plain, past the waving grass, to a dark shadow on the horizon. The hair on my arms stiffened. It hadn't been there last time I'd looked.

"Do you see it? There's something out there."

Swegde's eyes followed the path of my finger. "You're right. Looks like a herd of buffalo."

The sound grew louder, like thunder, but more guttural. "Is that what buffalo sound like?" I asked.

Swegde stared fixedly at the blotch of darkness, growing larger and closer.

"The scouting party are on horseback, right?" Even as the words came out of my mouth, I knew it wasn't them. I'd only sent out three men, and this looked like a whole battalion.

Swegde nodded. "Yes, but that's not what we're looking at." He was squinting hard, his lips pressed together.

"So, Buffalo?" I asked, trying to prompt Swegde to elaborate.

"No …" Swegde said slowly. "Buffalo don't move like that. It's men …"

I stared hard this time, trying to bring whatever it was into focus. *Still too far.* Then I heard the sound again, a great guttural cry, and fear caught my breath.

I knew exactly what I was looking at. It was men, all right —just not living ones. Barreling towards us was a great horde of draugr.

"Look." Swegde pointed to a speck, just in front of the charging undead.

The fear became ice in my veins. In front of the horde was a lone elf, running at a dead-out sprint.

"It's him," I said, jumping up. "We have to help."

I called Skalei to me, and charged into the plain.

I could hear the draugr calling now, their raspy voices in a full hunting chorus. In front of them raced the elf, hood over his head, cloak flying out behind him. I couldn't see his face, but I knew exactly who he was. And I had to get to him.

The draugr barreled after him, ravenous. Even as I ran towards him, I could tell that he wouldn't make it. The undead were simply too fast, too untiring. I had to do something.

Still sprinting, I drew Levateinn, Loki's wand. A weapon of the gods. Gripping it tightly, I tried to scribe a portal spell, but I was also running dead out. I missed a downward stroke and the spell sputtered, nothing more than a crackling burst of sparks. *Balls.*

I looked to the running elf. The draugr were almost upon him. I had to focus. Focusing was the only way I was going to save him.

Heart hammering, I skidded to a stop, then traced the spell precisely. My chest unclenched a little as a portal appeared in front of me. I leapt through.

I appeared a few feet in front of the elf I knew so well—and a few hundred feet in front of the draugr.

"Keep going!" I shouted, catching his eye. "I'll hold them off."

The draugr were bearing down on me, an army of the dead. I could hear their cries, smell the stench of their rotting bodies. If they got to me, they'd tear me to pieces. Maybe this hadn't been such a good idea.

Holding Levateinn in front of me like a sword, I planted my feet. Focusing, I slashed the shape of the rune *kaun*. I felt power build in the wand, and then a great gout of flame burst forth. The draugr's hunting cries turned to rasping screams as the fire tore into them. Their bodies blazed for a few moments, then burst like rancid fireworks.

But this horde was massive—more draugr than I'd ever seen in my life.

Standing before them, I kept scribing *kaun,* blasting any that came too close.

Swegde was shouting behind me. Moments later, flaming arrows began to trace the sky above my head as he fired into the horde. The fiery bolts ignited their dry and sinewy bodies. The monsters slowed as explosions rippled through their ranks.

"It's working!" I shouted.

I wielded Levateinn like a flamethrower, burning the draugr where they stood. They were calling to one another now, croaking shouts as they began retreating. I smiled. Even in their guttural voices, I heard fear.

Slowly they began to pick up speed, lumbering back into the vastness of the plains. I raced after them, burning any stragglers. A protective fury ignited my body, and the air smelled of smoke and death.

When I finally paused to catch my breath, the sun had set. Fires burned around me, and injured draugr moaned as vultures picked their bones. Warm light from their burning bodies danced over charred grasses.

A hand touched my shoulder.

"Ali, they're routed," said Swegde, his eyes gleaming in the darkness.

"Where did they come from?" I asked.

"The important thing is you defeated them, you were brilliant."

"They're still out there."

He stared into the distance. "We'll send riders to kill off the rest of them in the morning. You need to get back to the temple."

"Where is he?"

Swegde pointed behind me, to a cloaked figure couched in the grass. Forgetting my exhaustion, I ran to him.

"Ali?" his familiar voice warmed my chest.

Before I could yank his hood off myself, Barthol had wrapped me in one of his signature bear hugs.

"You're okay?" I asked. "Not hurt?"

"I'm fine. A bit tired though." Barthol tried to smile, but I could still see terror in his eyes. "I'm not used to running under the sun."

I looked at Barthol's outfit, heavy leather pants, a black cloak, and underneath—I frowned—his cave bear jacket. I was going to have to speak to him about the importance of function over style in a world with the sun.

"What happened to the other two scouts?" I asked.

He flinched. "Dead. Draugr ambushed us this morning."

"Oh my gods."

Barthol's eyes had gone unfocused, clearly reliving something terrible. I hugged him hard.

"It was awful, Ali. Awful …" My brother's arms tightened around me, and he rested his head on my shoulder for just a moment.

As I pulled away from him, I was already mentally reviewing his assignment, burying my emotional reaction. Just like Swegde taught me.

Swegde cleared his throat. "Tell us what you learned about the draugr." By his abrupt tone, it was clear he thought we did not have time for Barthol's emotions. "Are they the ones who were stealing our cattle?"

Barthol tried to school his features into something manly. "The draugr are everywhere in the west."

"How many?" Swegde barked.

"Thousands upon thousands. In some places the plains are nearly black with their bodies. Vultures everywhere … the smell …" He shuddered visibly.

"Oh gods," said Swegde under his breath. "You saw this with your eyes?"

Barthol nodded.

"Where did they come from?" I asked.

Barthol shook his head. "No idea. They just stretched back to the horizon. There were so many … There was no way to pass through them to find out."

"So just the western plains?" Swegde asked hopefully.

Barthol's expression looked pained. "No, they're on the move. Headed this way. I think we have a week at best before they're at the gates of Vanaheim."

Swegde paled. "I need to warn the tribes." He paused, looking to me for permission.

"Yes, of course, Swegde," I said. "Go ahead. I'm going to walk back with Barthol. I've got the wand to protect us."

Swegde nodded. "All right, Ali. I'll see you in the temple in an hour."

"Can you organize a meeting of the council?"

"Of course."

As Swegde hurried off into the night, I turned back to Barthol. "Are you sure you're not hurt?"

"I'm fine. I was able to escape, when—" Barthol grimaced. "When the draugr were eating. I'm fine. Just really tired." He faltered, and I caught him by the elbow, helping him balance.

"Take your time, brother."

We walked in silence for a while along the edge of the forest, the stars gleaming above us. It was a perfectly clear night, and I could see the Milky Way, the thousands upon thousands of stars that still felt so new and alien.

"Did you ever think you'd be walking under the stars like this?" I asked.

Barthol shook his head, half smiling. "They're so beautiful."

"Did you know they have names?" I continued, keeping the subject away from draugr. "That group of stars over there, it's called Aurvandil's Toe, and that one there is Karl-vagn, the soldier's chariot."

"How do you know all this?"

"Swegde told me."

Barthol's eyebrows flicked up, and he grinned knowingly. "Swegde? Is he your boyfriend?"

I rolled my eyes. "Definitely not."

Barthol's grin spread wider. "But have you seen his arms? They're like tree trunks."

"No brother, he's just a close advisor. He was the Regent, he knows the most about the Vanir."

"You should see how he looks at you, when he goes on about bear wrestling."

"Barthol!" I said sharply. I wasn't in the mood. "I'm the

Empress now. Boyfriends aren't a thing, and I don't think of Swegde that way."

I thought of what the Norn had told me: *Your duty is bigger than you are. There are great snarls in the Wyrd for you to untangle; both your peoples need your full attention if they are to survive.*

"So you're still thinking of him, aren't you?" asked Barthol.

"Galin? Of course not," I lied. "The Norn broke the soul bond, at my request. Because that's not real love, is it? It's just magic." My chest felt tight, breathless.

What I didn't tell him was that when I severed the mating bond, I'd hoped we'd get to know each other in a normal way. Not that we'd never see each other again. I'd never meant for this to happen.

"Do you really think he survived?" asked Barthol quietly.

"He's Galin. He's definitely alive." It came out sounding too sharp, angry. "I checked the bottom of the Well of Wyrd myself, there was no *body—*" For some annoying reason my voice decided to crack as I said *body.*

"Or that giant squirrel you told me about carried him off and ate him." Barthol's eyes gleamed in the darkness. "Ali, I think he's gone. If he wanted to speak to you, he'd find a way to communicate. He of all people could do that."

I didn't reply. My chest ached sharply. The constellations no longer seemed interesting; the night had become almost oppressive.

Maybe Barthol was right. I had to believe he was still alive, but maybe he didn't want to see me. He was the most powerful sorcerer the world had ever known. If he wanted to get a message to me, he would've found a way by now.

CHAPTER 2

GALIN

From my throne, I stared out into the vastness of Hela's dark hall. In ancient alcoves, votive candles cast wavering light over the flagstone floor and columns.

Just as I had done a minute ago, just as I had done an hour earlier, just as I had done the day before. I was familiar with every broken stone, every chipped column, every pile of dust and bone. The only thing that changed was the position of the shades. Sometimes there were hundreds floating around, other times only a few, but never were there none.

I closed my eyes, ready to ascend to the astral plane. This was my only escape from this world. In the astral realm, I could scan the souls of the living. When I first arrived in Hel, I'd visited the plane every hour. I had one purpose then, to check on Ali's soul, to make sure she was safe.

In those early days here, I'd felt broken. I'd been king of the High Elves, ready to lead them to a better world. I'd had a mate I loved, a beautiful Night Elf with eyes that shone like molten silver.

And in just a matter of hours, I'd lost it all.

My mate had broken the bond. My sister had stabbed me, sending me into the Well of Wyrd.

If it weren't for Hela, the Goddess of Death, I'd be dead.

She'd come for me as I breathed my last breaths. She healed me, brought me to Hel to join her on the throne as king.

And that's exactly what I'd become: the King of Shades, the King of Darkness … the King of Nothing. That last title was most accurate—my heart was empty, my soul lost. There were times when I'd thought of sending a message to Ali, but what would be the point? She'd severed our soul mate bond. It was over now.

As I tried to recall that sharp pain I'd felt when I first arrived here, I felt … nothing. My heart had started to turn dark and withered. I wasn't a lich, but I might as well have been. My body was a husk—ashes and dust in my chest.

"Galin?"

I opened my eyes to see the Queen of Hel peering at me from her throne.

"Yes, your Highness?" I might be the King of Hel, but Hela was a goddess—a daughter of Loki.

My queen was beautiful and terrifying to behold—swirls of dark blue tattoos over the right half of her body. The other half was white as a lake of ice. Long, black hair draped over a white gown. She was stunning in an eerie way. Elegant. Her dark eyes shone with ruthless intelligence.

She was more dangerous than I ever could have imagined.

"I need satisfaction," she breathed in a husky voice.

Hela was my queen, and I was her king, but I didn't desire her.

"I am indisposed." An obvious lie. I hadn't done anything in weeks, and I'd been telling her this lie since I got here.

Fortunately, Hela never seemed to care.

She shrugged. "Then entertain me, King."

I sighed. "How shall I do that, my Goddess? I am not an entertaining person."

"I don't care. Get out of your chair. Tell me a story, sing me a song, take off your shirt and dance for me. It doesn't matter, as long as you do something to end this monotony."

I gripped the stone arms of the throne. "If you could visit the Nastrand, you could breathe in the scent of the sea."

"You know I cannot leave this place. The iron walls, they are the prison of the gods. Their magic binds me to these stones. And besides, I must rule over my people—"

"The shades?" The shades were hardly people, and they definitely didn't need ruling. They seemed happy to float over the cold mud, or hover above the stones of Hela's throne room, whispering quietly to one another.

"They are people to me."

"Perhaps you could ask *them* to entertain you, then." Irritation laced my tone.

She turned away from me. "Ganglati," she said sharply. "What news do you have?"

My old friend appeared in front of us, a large shade with pale eyes.

"The shades report mist and rain, and eight hours ago a stone fell from the ceiling." He spoke in a hushed, reverent tone. "The first in a hundred years. There was quite a to-do about it."

"No, you fool, tell me of the worlds beyond the iron walls." Her voice boomed, echoing in the vast hall. "What do you hear from Midgard? What about Vanaheim? What of the humans and the elves?"

Ganglati seemed unperturbed by Hela's tone. "Ah. My Queen, terror reigns in the worlds of the living. Since you closed the gates to Hel, the dead that walk Helvegr have been turning round. Great hordes roam the plains of Vanaheim. They are hungry, and they feast on men and elves alike."

A thin tendril of dread curled through me—concern for the living. Was I actually *feeling* something again?

"Good," said Hela, her affect flat. "The more we send away, the more quickly they will grow in number—"

"Hela," I cut in, my blood heating. "Why do you torture the mortals by letting the dead lay waste to their lands?"

Hela laughed, a strange guttural sound that set my teeth on edge. "You underestimate me, my King. I have a plan to escape, to rule the nine realms. My father's wand—"

"No," I interrupted. "Even if you had Levateinn, it would not be enough to break you out. It cannot tear down the walls. You are trapped here until the end of time."

"You are right that I am trapped here." Hela's dark eyes searched my own.

A strange sensation trickled down my spine, one that I rarely felt—it took me a moment to recognize it as fear.

She crossed to me, stepping up onto the dais, then leaned down and gripped the collar of my shirt. She ripped it open. "But I wasn't thinking Levateinn was the only tool I'd use to escape, or that I'd be the first to leave these walls."

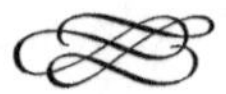

CHAPTER 3

ALI

With Barthol by my side, we crossed through the towering halls of golden stone. Arches swept high above us, and moonlight spilled onto the floor.

My brother flashed me a tired smile. "You could have been a dictator instead of bothering with the council."

"No, Barthol. I'm trying to do things differently. I don't want to be an asshole leader. I'm not King Gorm." When I took over as high leader of the tribes of elves, the first thing I'd done was create a council of advisors, so every tribe would be represented. I asked each one to send me two members to represent their interests—the Night Elves, the Vanir, and the High Elves.

My footfalls echoed off the stone, and I glanced at my brother again. He looked exhausted. His hair lay matted to his forehead, and his boots were caked with mud. I knew I should let him shower and clean up, but I wanted to talk to him before the meeting.

"I was worried about you," I said, touching his arm. "That was way too close. If Swegde and I hadn't been waiting for you, you'd be draugr food now."

Barthol laughed. "You don't need to worry about me, sis."

I glowered at him. "You were wearing your cave bear jacket. It was hot out. Someone needs to teach you common sense."

"I know what I'm doing. It's my lucky jacket."

"Look, I know you want a role for yourself, but getting eaten by draugr is not the one I had in mind."

Barthol's jaw tightened. "Can I have a role on the council then?"

I shook my head. "You're my brother, it will be nepotism if I put you on the council."

"Harald and Sigre are brother and sister representatives."

"Yes, that is true, but they're High Elves, and you're a Night Elf. We need Vanir to represent the Vanir. Obviously."

"They trust me to scout for them," he said irritably, picking up his pace toward the council hall.

"Barthol." I hurried to catch up. "I'm the Empress, and I have to lead in a way that builds trust."

"And I'm your humble servant." He opened the door, giving me an exaggerated bow.

"Please do not be melodramatic right now. You're embarrassing me, as usual," I muttered.

I stepped into the council chamber, a large room with a heavy oak table in the center and a large fireplace at the far end. Swegde sat at the table, drinking wine with the Night Elves—Bo, and Lynheid.

Barthol dropped into one of the chairs by the fire, sulking.

Ignoring him, I turned to one of the Vanir guards at the door. "Can you see that Barthol gets something to eat and drink?" I said quietly. "He's had a very long day."

The guard nodded and slipped into the hall.

As I crossed to the council table, Bo straightened. "What's this all about?"

"When Harald and Sigre arrive I will explain everything."

Bo yawned, rubbing his eyes. "It had better be important. I was sleeping."

"It is, trust me."

I sat, but only briefly, as Harald and Sigre pushed open the door a minute later. Even though I saw them frequently now, I couldn't help but stare. It was nearly three in the morning, but both were immaculately dressed, in black velvet robes that shimmered slightly in the firelight. While King Gorm had been flamboyant, with an obsession with food and gold, these elves were considerably more austere.

Harald was an unusually tall elf, thin and narrow, like he'd been born small and subsequently stretched out on a rack. Sigre had pale gold hair that she wore in a tight bun on the top of her head. While not as tall as her brother, she had long arms and legs, which made her look a bit like an insect.

From the other side of the table, she stared at me with narrowed eyes. A praying mantis, I decided. If I turned my back I was certain she would try to bite my head off.

"It appears we now have a quorum," said Bo. "What is so important you needed to rouse me out of a dream about my harem?"

Bo had become a thorn in my side. And of course he had —even if we'd been in prison together, he'd never forgiven me for threatening his life. And now, he looked absolutely ridiculous with his slicked-down hair and black suit—full of self-importance.

"One of my scouts—"

"Your brother, you mean," Bo grumbled.

Gods, this man clearly needed a solid eight hours of shut-eye.

"Bo, why don't you drink some of this nice wine? You are clearly cranky." *Everyone* was cranky.

"Don't patronize me Ali—"

I leaned forward, meeting his gaze. "Don't patronize me

Empress. And I would not have woken you up unless it was deadly important. Barthol has returned from a scouting mission. He's brought with him urgent news you all need to hear." I gestured to Barthol, indicating he should speak.

Barthol rose from his chair by the fire. He rubbed a hand across his face, looking absolutely exhausted. "I just returned from the western plains."

"On your own?" Bo said sharply.

"There were three of us—"

"Then where are the other two?"

"Dead. I will explain if you let me speak, Bo."

Bo smoothed his slick hair. "All right. Tell us what happened."

"We traveled west for two days, but then the draugr became too numerous to continue." Barthol drew in a deep breath. "We rode until we reached the Sapphire Hills. When we climbed to the top, we saw a great horde of draugr gathering, hundreds of thousands of them, grunting and calling."

"How do you know they were draugr and not elves or men?" said Bo.

Barthol's throat bobbed. "Well, for one thing they ate the elves and horses I was with."

"All right." Bo's voice cracked. "So we'll send an army to fight them. The creatures aren't intelligent."

"If I may speak," Harald cut in, "part of Boston is overrun with draugr. We've been sending soldiers armed with torches to burn them for years, but we've only succeeded in losing men."

"What have you heard from the Shadow Caverns?" Sigre asked. "Our spies have all gone silent."

"Your spies?" snapped Bo. "What are you doing spying on Night Elves when we are allied?"

"Bo," I snarled. "Just answer her question."

Bo crossed his arms over his chest, but he answered Sigre.

"The Shadow Caverns have gone silent. I've sent a number of messengers, but none of them have returned."

I raised my hands. "It is clear we have a serious draugr problem. Both here in Vanaheim and possibly in the Shadow Caverns too. I brought you all here, not because I wanted you to fight with each other, but because I wanted to develop a plan to fight the undead. Does anyone have any suggestions?"

The table fell silent, and Bo glared at the High Elves.

At last Swegde leaned forward. "We need to join forces and defend ourselves. Together we might stand a chance. Fighting alone, we'll all be overrun. We need to pick a single defensible position, one that the draugr can't easily penetrate."

"The Citadel," said Harald.

I nodded. The Citadel had kept Marroc caged for a thousand years, it could keep the draugr out.

When I thought of him, I felt as if my heart were twisting, and I could no longer focus.

"The Citadel," I repeated, thinking of how Marroc had looked when I first met him.

"Then it's decided." Harald stood.

"Actually I was thinking of the temple," said Swegde. "The city walls can easily hold all three tribes of elves. The Citadel is already surrounded by bloodthirsty draugr, as you have mentioned, Harald. Our temple is not."

Of course, that made sense. And I would have thought of it if I hadn't been distracted by thinking of Galin—Marroc as he'd been known then. This was why Swegde was right: to be an effective leader, you couldn't let your emotions rule you. You had to *smother* them, or people would die.

I cleared my throat. "Of course. Good point. I suggest we plan to relocate our tribes here. But then we need to figure out what to do about the draugr."

Swegde frowned. "We'll fight them."

"Right," said Bo, "but for how long? Months? Years? If we want to defeat them we'll need to learn where they're coming from, and why there are so many."

Swegde shrugged. "There'll be time for that. For now we try to kill as many of them as possible."

"No," I said. "Bo has a point. Just killing the draugr may not be enough to defeat them. We should find out where they're coming from, or they may not stop." I pinched the bridge of my nose, closing my eyes to try to think clearly. "We can't cross the western plains. There were too many of them. But there has got to be a way …"

I cursed under my breath. If I knew a bit more magic, I could ascend to the astral plane, or whatever Galin had called it. I could search for the source of the draugr hordes from the safety of my room. But I didn't know how to do that. In fact, I only knew two spells: fire and portals.

Just as I was trying to formulate my thoughts, a strange scratching noise rose from the fireplace.

Barthol whirled to stare at it.

"It sounds like an animal," whispered Sigre.

"Probably a bird," said Bo. "They fly down chimneys sometimes."

"But not when there's a fire burning," said Harald. He stood next to Sigre, a silver dagger gleaming in his hand.

A great cloud of soot and sparks erupted from the fireplace, and a large raven burst into the room, with dark magic spilling from its body.

CHAPTER 4

ALI

The raven circled the room, squawking. Then suddenly it landed in the center of the table. It cocked its head, fixing me with a beady eye.

Swegde drew his sword, and it glinted in the firelight.

The raven began to hop towards me, its talons clacking on the old wood. I pointed Skalei at it. Ravens were sacred, but the stench of decay curled from it, and shadows thickened the air around it.

With a shout, Swegde lunged, slashing with his sword, but the bird hopped above the blade and began flying around the room again.

Barthol sidled up to me, as Sigre began screaming, "It's a harbinger of death. We're all going to die!"

The raven landed on the top of a door frame, squawking angrily at Swegde. Swegde stalked towards it, ready to slash at it again. But even as he did, the bird fixed its gaze on me, black eyes flashing with a keen intelligence that did not belong to a bird.

The hair on my arms stiffened. I stepped back. And yet, even as I did so I felt my fear wane.

Something about the bird seemed familiar. Ravens were

the messengers of the gods, and Galin had once told me that he'd kept them as pets. And as for the dark magic? Maybe that reminded me of Galin, too.

Stop thinking about him, Ali. Stop. Thinking. About. Galin.

As I tried to collect my thoughts, Lynheid stepped forward. Her silvery Night Elf eyes shone as she stared at the raven. She pointed to it. "I believe the creature has a package tied to its leg."

I frowned. Sure enough, tied just above its right foot was a small leather pouch.

"Just give me a moment to kill it," said Swegde, lifting his sword over his head.

"No, wait!" I shouted, and Swegde lowered his sword. "Killing isn't always the answer to everything, Swegde. Put your sword away."

The bird cocked its head, and I had the disturbing sense that it could understand what I was saying. Fixing me again with its beady black eyes, it flew across the room and landed on the table in front of me.

It stared at me unblinking, darkness staining the air around it.

"I promise I won't hurt you," I said softly.

The raven moved closer. It squawked again, so loudly I winced. Then, as delicately as a house cat looking to get petted, it stepped into my hand.

I heard Sigre breathe in sharply, but the bird curled its head under a wing.

Carefully, I undid the leather ties that held the pouch closed. Inside was a small piece of parchment. As soon as I drew it out, the raven leapt into the air, flying around the room and screeching. Then, it flew into the fireplace, leaving us once more in the quiet.

"That raven was cursed," Sigre whispered. "Someone in this room has a black hex."

Ignoring the High Elf princess, I unrolled the parchment. As I read the letter, a strange sensation washed over me. It was as if I couldn't quite breathe; my heart pounded too hard in my chest.

"What does it say? Who sent it?" asked Bo, leaning over my shoulder.

I shifted away from him. "It's from Galin."

A hush fell over the room. Sigre and Harald exchanged a look. Bo cursed under his breath.

"The sorcerer is dead," said Harald at last. "We all saw Revna stab him before he fell into the Well of Wyrd. There is no way he could have survived."

"But he's Galin." An edge undercut my voice. "Of course he isn't dead."

I read the letter out loud.

Dear Ali,

I rule here as King of Hel. I am consort to Hela, Goddess of the Dead. She is the reason the draugr invade the mortal lands. She will stop at nothing until she escapes Hel's iron walls. If you free me, I can help defeat the draugr.

—Galin.

"Consort?" I shouted at the end.

"Ali," said Swegde. "Focus."

I squeezed my eyes shut, my emotions whirling. On the one hand, Galin was alive, and he was offering to help us. This was what I'd been waiting to hear all this time.

On the other hand, he'd had the ability to contact me all this time, and didn't. Just like Barthol said.

And what was more—he'd been banging a goddess. A *goddess*. What did she look like now that she was alive? Beautiful, I imagined.

I stared for far too long at the way he'd signed it. Not a

love, not even a *yours*. Just a slash across the page. I gritted my teeth and lifted my eyes to the others, forcing my emotions under the surface.

I'd done this. I'd severed the mating bond. What did I expect? It was the magical version of a break up. And now he was banging a goddess.

My fists clenched. *Stop thinking about Galin.*

"Well," laughed Sigre. "No one living knows how to get to Hel. Clearly this is a forgery."

"Actually, I have visited Hel," I said quietly.

Sigre's eyes widened, and she stared at me like I might be a draugr in disguise.

"That's impossible," said Harald.

I held up Levateinn. "Where do you think I got this?"

Sigre crossed her arms. "Even if she visited Hel, she did it with the sorcerer's help."

"That is true," said Bo.

My throat felt tight. "We are being offered help by the King of Hel. I think we should take it."

Only Swegde spoke. "It's extremely risky ..."

"Does anyone else have a better idea for defeating the draugr?" I asked.

Barthol's eyes lit up. "I've been thinking we could build enormous catapults. Then we could launch Molotov cocktails ..."

But as my brother spoke, I found myself thinking about Galin again.

If you free me ...

So he'd chosen not to contact me, but maybe he didn't have a choice about much else. Clearly, he was trapped there —and he needed us to let him out.

We needed him, too. If anyone could stop the draugr hordes, it was him. He'd been able to imprison the Night Elves behind a magic wall for more than a thousand years. If

I freed him, maybe he could do the same thing to the draugr. Or he could help kill them. He was the only one who could really use Loki's wand.

"I should go to Hel," I said, interrupting Barthol's in-depth description of a Molotov cocktail.

Barthol stared at me. "But it's impossible. Last time you visited, you nearly drowned on the way. You were attacked by the Nokk and had to climb over the iron wall. Why would you go back?"

This was the point where I really began to regret telling Barthol about my adventures with Galin—back when Galin had been Marroc. The journey sounded terrifying, when in fact—

Actually he was right. It had been terrifying. But still, I had to try.

I heaved a deep breath. "Traveling over the waterfall and through the subterranean lake would be risky." I bit my lip. "But I don't have to travel that way this time."

"What do you mean?" asked Barthol.

"Well, we were on our way to steal Levateinn last time." I held up the wand. "But now that I've got it—I can create a portal. It's one of the only things I know how to do with this wand. I might as well put it to use."

"You can make a portal into Hel?" Sigre gasped with terror. "I don't think this is a good idea."

"I think I can make the portal. I mean I've never actually tried—but it shouldn't be any more difficult than making any other portal. The crucial thing is that I've been there before, so conjuring the portal is possible."

"But what will happen after that?" asked Barthol.

My nerves buzzed at the thought of seeing him again. "I'll step through and go find Galin. I'll try to avoid his ... *queen.* I'll have the wand, so I can return to Vanaheim any time."

Dangerous as it was to steal a consort from a death

goddess, this idea was making more and more sense. In fact, the fear in my gut had been replaced by a thrilling excitement. Across the table I could see Barthol's eyes gleaming as well.

"I'll go with you!" he exclaimed.

"Absolutely not," said Swegde.

"Why not?" Bo leaned forward. "I don't think it's a good idea if she goes alone."

"Clearly," said Barthol. "And I should be the one to go. I'm her brother. We've done plenty of jobs together already."

Like the time you left me in the Silfarson's bank to be nearly eaten by a draugr, attacked by a troll, and imprisoned by the High Elves.

But really—Barthol had a point. "Having a second person along could be helpful," I said. "And I trust Barthol."

"What if you get separated?" asked Swegde. "And one of you can't return?"

"Then this could come in handy." Lynheid drew a vergr crystal from under the folds of her dress. "I can bind it to Barthol."

I grinned. "Oh brilliant idea."

"I don't understand," said Harald.

"Vergr crystals allow for teleportation," I explained. "We can leave it here in Vanaheim, so that if we run into any trouble he can be instantly transported out of Hel. And I've got my own crystal, and Levateinn. I'll make a portal back here when it's time to go."

"I don't like this idea," said Harald, his voice icy. "Can we really trust this traitor—someone who turned against his own family? I think he's more likely to murder us than to help us."

"Yes," I snapped. "We can trust him."

"Ali's right," said Swegde. "His skills as a sorcerer are legendary. We need his help, or the draugr will overwhelm us eventually. We need to close the doors to Hel. The dead outnumber us by legions, and we can't throw Molotov cocktails forever."

"Then it's settled," I said. "As soon as Barthol is bound to the crystal, we'll leave—"

"No," Sigre barked. "It is not settled. I object."

Harald straightened. "As do I."

"On what grounds?" growled Swegde, clearly out of patience.

"He can't be trusted," Harald hissed.

As I stared at him, it hit me like a fist. Why hadn't I thought of it before? Galin was the rightful ruler of Midgard. Harald was only ruling in his absence.

"Obviously, the council must vote." Sigre flicked her pale hair over her shoulder. "You are, after all, not a dictator. Isn't that what you said? Those are the rules. And since it's your proposal, you must abstain from voting. Or have you changed your mind?"

"Fine," I said through gritted teeth. Clearly, being a dictator was easier.

"All right." Swegde held up his hands. "Harald, how do you vote?"

"Absolutely not."

"Sigre?"

"No."

Swegde looked to Lynheid, who seemed to be hiding behind her silver hair.

"Yes," she said quietly.

"And I'm also a yes," said Swegde. That made two *No's* and two *Yes's*. All our eyes turned to Bo—the tie-breaking vote.

Bo adjusted his lapels. "Is this perhaps because you're hoping to mate with him again? Are you sure you're doing this for the right reasons? You're not letting your emotions get the best of you, are you?"

Anger erupted in my mind. "The Norn severed the connection between our souls. I feel nothing for him. I am the Empress of the Vanir, leader of the elves. My only duty is to my people. Galin means nothing to me anymore."

I held my breath as Bo stared at me for a long time, then looked to Swegde. "Well I don't have any better suggestions. I vote yes."

I exhaled, wondering why I felt this wild sense of giddiness.

After all—I *had* severed the bond. What was left?

CHAPTER 5

ALI

Two hours later, Barthol and I stood in the main hall of the Vanir temple, sandstone vaults in sharp peaks high above us.

I was dressed in my full assassin's outfit: close-fitting leather pants and jacket, Levateinn at my hip. Barthol also wore leather pants, but instead of a tight jacket he'd chosen to go with his cave bear coat. Because of course he did.

He'd also grabbed a small sword, even though I told him it would be useless against the shades.

Rolling my shoulders, I drew Levateinn. I studied the silver wand for a long moment. I had spent every day of the last month practicing the two spells I knew: fire and portal.

I glanced at Barthol. "Do you remember how to invoke your vergr crystal?"

He nodded.

"Good. If anything goes wrong I want you to call it right away, okay? We are basically stealing from a death goddess."

"I got it Ali."

I wanted to say that Barthol wasn't nearly as experienced as me, that Hel was extremely dangerous and he needed to do exactly what I said, but I bit my tongue. I needed to trust him, not distract him with being patronized.

I took in a deep breath. "All right, I'm going to open the portal now."

As I scribed the portal spell, and streaks of light beamed before me, Barthol stepped back.

I sharpened my focus. The trick to making it work, I'd learned, was to envision exactly where you wanted to go. It was why you could only go someplace you'd already been. So as I incanted the runes, I tried to remember the tunnel that led to Hela's tomb. I mostly remembered that it had been at the base of the cliff—a crack in a sheer cliff of stark gray rock.

And this was where the first problem presented itself.

As much as I tried to recall specific details, I wasn't sure I'd gotten a good look at that part of the cliff. Had I?

I squeezed my eyes tight, trying to bring up the image: gray clouds, black mud, jagged stone rising high, high above me.

Then, with an electric pop, the portal appeared in front of me. The wand thrummed in my hand, strangely heavy. I didn't know how long I could keep the portal open.

"You go first, I'll be right behind you," I said to Barthol.

I concentrated as my brother stepped through and disappeared with the sound of crackling static.

I stared at the shimmering surface of the portal. This was it; I was going back to Hel. The realm of mud, mist, shades, and death. I should have been worried, scared even, but instead I was strangely excited. A sort of nervous energy radiated through my body—a bit like when I'd first opened the note from Galin.

For an instant I pictured his face vividly: square jaw, sharp cheekbones, golden eyes. What would it be like to see him again? Had he missed me at all?

Only one way to find out.

Gripping the wand, I stepped through the portal.

I gasped as cold rain sprayed my face and instantly soaked my hair. All around me rain poured down, like being under a shower that was set on cold and turned up to max spray. My feet squelched in black mud when I stepped forward.

"Ali, over here," Barthol called out.

In the icy deluge, I tried to wipe the water from my face with the sleeve of my leather jacket. Already I regretted my decision to wear it. I pressed a hand to my forehead like a sort of visor, trying to look for my brother in the dim light.

"Here," he said again.

At last, I saw him. He stood with his back against a wall of gray rock. Jagged stone jutted out above him, giving him some protection from the rain. But on either side, streams of water poured down from the top of the cliff high above.

Bingo. I'd got us to the right spot. At least I thought so.

I hurried over and squeezed in next to him under the overhang of rock.

"I didn't realize it rained so much in Hel." Barthol hugged himself, teeth chattering, his cave bear jacket giving off a dead-animal smell.

"Neither did I. Last time it was mostly just a thick mist and fog." I shivered as an ice-cold rivulet of water dripped down my back.

"Do you know where we are?" he asked.

I grimaced. "I tried to send us to the entrance of Hela's tomb."

"What's it look like?"

With a growing sense of unease, I peered around. The rain was pouring down in thick sheets, pooling in deep puddles on the black mud. "The entrance was a big crack in the cliff."

"I don't see anything like that," said Barthol. "Just rock."

Neither did I. *Shit.*

Already I was nearly soaked through, my leather pants sticking to my legs unpleasantly. I really wanted to get out of the rain.

"Do you know the way?" Barthol asked hopefully.

Again, I looked in either direction along the wall of rock. I didn't recognize anything. "No. But let's try going right and see what happens."

Slowly we began to walk along the base of the cliff. Black muck sucked at my feet, and I wished I'd thought to wear rubber boots. My shoes were already soaked through.

"Ali." Barthol grabbed my shoulder. "What *is* that?"

He pointed behind us to a dark shape in the mist, and my stomach dropped. It hung like a dark stain over the ground, and the rain simply passed through it. Unquestionably, one of the local denizens.

"It's a shade," I whispered. "Don't give him any attention."

I grabbed his wrist, pulling him forward, away from the shadowy spirit.

We continued along the base of the cliff, but found only sheer rock. Where was the entrance to Hela's tomb? I stopped to look back, hoping the shade had wandered off, but the thing still lingered in the air. Was it following us?

I turned to walk again, but Barthol called my name.

"Ali, look." He pointed at something in the rock farther ahead—a dark space at the very bottom of the cliff. I hurried until I reached it.

There, at knee level, was a small entrance, large enough for a child. It definitely wasn't the crack I remembered, but it was an opening nonetheless.

"I think it's a cave," said Barthol.

If there was one thing the Night Elves understood, it was caves.

I nodded, crouching down to poke my head inside a dark, narrow tunnel. It wasn't the path I'd taken before. But what I liked about it right now was its distinct and total lack of ice-cold rain.

"I think we should try it," I said, pulling my head out to talk to Barthol. "Maybe it will lead to Galin."

My brother nodded. "I just want to get out of this rain."

I crawled inside. Barthol grunted as he squeezed in behind me.

I pushed my wet hair off my face. The cave was even narrower than I'd anticipated, with a ceiling so low, we were forced to crawl on hands and knees. But it was dry! In fact, it was strangely warm. *Bonus.*

As Night Elves, we were basically at home here in the claustrophobic dark, able to see in the pitch black.

"Just to clarify," said Barthol. "You have no idea where this goes?"

"No idea," I said.

As I crawled forward, the cave remained narrow. I realized it was nearly circular, like a tube. Was it man made?

After another hundred yards, nothing had changed. Just as I was starting to worry that we'd have to turn back, I saw a light.

"There's something ahead of us," I whispered.

"I see it too."

I wriggled on my stomach, until I was able to see a sort of grate in the floor. Light streamed through, drawing lines of light and shadow on the ceiling of the tunnel. We were in some kind of air vent.

I carefully peeked through. Below me was a lavishly decorated bedroom. A large king-sized bed with a white duvet, a fireplace at the far end, and a sofa that faced a row of tall windows. Biting my lip, I wondered if this was where Galin's goddess-consorting duties took place …

Had he been a willing participant?

I clenched my jaw. It didn't matter. That wasn't why I was here.

Yet the prospect of seeing him again got my heart racing. Peering around the room, I saw two doors, one across from the bed and another closer to the fireplace.

Barthol brushed against me, trying to get a look. "What is it?"

"A bedroom."

"Galin's?" Barthol said, a little too loudly.

I clamped my hand over his mouth and pointed at the door by the fireplace. Just as he'd started to speak, I'd seen it move.

His eyes widened. Together we watched as the door slowly creaked open.

I couldn't see anything at first. Just a huge cloud of some sort of ghostly white mist. The scent of lavender floated through the air, and the sound of a faucet running. The mist was steam from a shower or bath.

The steam billowed into the bedroom. Then, silhouetted within it, a tall figure appeared. Not large and broad shouldered, but lithe and thin.

I nearly gasped as I saw blue, swirling tattoos against icy skin. The Goddess of the Dead. Strangely beautiful, she stepped into her bedroom.

Jealousy and a kind of possessiveness pierced my heart. Had she seduced Galin? Or trapped him?

Interlacing her fingers, she stretched her arms above her head, looking at herself in the mirror.

When I'd seen the goddess before, she'd been basically mummified. A desiccated corpse in moldering robes propped up on an old throne. Now she was *stunning,* her body perfection, her hair a silky onyx.

I stole a glance at Barthol. He had gone completely still,

and his eyes bulged so wildly they looked like they might pop out of his head.

Hela slipped a thin robe of pale silk over her shoulders. She shook her hair out, then strode from the room.

"Whoa, whoa, whoa," Barthol breathed out. "*Who* was that?"

"Did you see her blue and ivory skin?"

"Hela," he whispered. "She is perfect."

"I mean, she's okay, I guess," I said sourly. "She may have trapped Galin here against his will, you know."

"Hela …" Barthol echoed, his eyes wide as dinner plates.

Rolling my eyes, I started to crawl forward. When I'd gone a few yards I twisted around to check on Barthol. He still stared through the grate.

"Barthol," I whispered sharply, "we have to keep moving."

"Hela …" Barthol said again, in a slow monotone.

"Snap out of it bro," I said in my best big-sister voice. "She's a goddess, and she's out of your league."

At last, he started moving again.

"She was totally naked," he whispered.

"I noticed. Can you get a grip? We both know you've had plenty of women. What was that elf's name, the one you met at the mushroom harvest last year? She was totally cute. I know you and she had a little thing together. Hela is forcing Galin to be here against his will, and unleashing draugr into the world of the living. Red flags, my friend. Red flags."

Barthol nodded, even as his expression remained vacant. "Do you think I'll get to meet her?"

"No," I snapped.

Because if we met Hela, that would mean that something had gone very wrong, and our chances of making it out of here would dwindle to nothing.

CHAPTER 6

ALI

 arthol and I continued through the tunnel, crossing over more grates—none with naked goddesses, much to my relief. Barthol stopped to peer into each one of them just in case. We passed a couple of storerooms, and an empty hallway lit by purple flames.

As we moved deeper into the ventilation tunnel, the air got warmer. My pants and jacket began to dry, which was nice. Assuming we weren't heading for a giant flaming fireplace.

My chest tightened as I saw a barrier up ahead—a horizontal grate at the end of the tunnel. If anyone looked through at this point, they would see us.

Crawling on my stomach, I inched towards it until I could peer through the metal.

This time, I recognized the room on the other side. It was Hela's tomb, the place where Ganglati and the shades had taken Galin and me when we first entered Hel—a hall of enormous rock and vaulted ceilings. Warm light from candles in alcoves danced back and forth over the stones and the piles of bones. What a gloomy place.

Hela's crumbling throne was empty, but standing in front of it, his back to me, was a familiar form. I would have recognized his powerful warrior's body anywhere. And yet he wasn't the same Galin—not at all.

Shirtless, his chest was marked with inky runes that snaked over his thickly corded muscles. Instead of the golden blond hair I'd last seen, his hair had returned to black. But the most concerning thing about him was the dark vapor drifting around him—like the shadow magic around the raven.

He turned and strode towards a door beside the throne. For an instant, I caught a glimpse of his profile, and I drew in an involuntary breath at his unearthly beauty. There were the familiar sharp cheekbones, sculpted by shadows, his masculine jawline.

I wanted to talk to him. Why did this dark sorcerer in Hel still feel kind of like home?

Staring at his beautiful face, all the time we'd spent together came back to me in a flash: climbing the wall of the Citadel, the battle in Boston Common, running my hands over his chest in the Well of Wyrd.

He seemed so familiar, and yet entirely alien. Back then, we had a soul bond, and I'd been inextricably drawn to him, like the proverbial moth to a flame.

Now—I reminded myself—he was just another elf. Not my mate. He was just a very, very beautiful elf who I felt nothing for except a sharp squeezing in my heart and extreme excitement, a racing pulse—

Stop it, Ali.

I wondered again if I'd done the right thing, but the bottom line was—if he didn't love me without magic, then it was never real, was it? It was like mind control. I'd needed to know the truth.

Forcing myself to focus, I scanned the empty hall. Unfortunately it wasn't empty; shades drifted about slowly, like motes in still air. As much as I wanted to jump down and run after Galin, that wasn't possible.

Barthol slid up next to me. "Hela seemed lonely," he whispered.

"I will murder you with the wand if you don't stop talking about her. She's had Galin to keep her company, anyway. She would chew through you like a starved leech. There'd be nothing left but a dried-up corpse. She's bad news. Anyway, our goal here is to talk to Galin. I just saw him slip through that door next to the throne. We need to find a way to get over there to follow him. Any ideas?"

He stared through the grate. "We could just make a run for it?"

I shook my head, wondering why I'd brought him. "The shades will see us as soon as we step out of this tunnel. And if I create a portal to where he was standing, they'll notice. What about a diversion? When the shades are distracted, I can create a portal that opens near where Galin was headed."

"Oh good idea." Barthol's eyebrows flicked up, and I hoped his next idea wouldn't involve Molotov cocktails and catapults. "What if you made a fire?" He pointed at Levateinn on my hip.

Not a bad idea. "That works."

I drew Levateinn and began to conjure the fire spell. A moment later a small gout of flame burst out of the wand and into the great hall. It began to burn on the stone just in front of our vent.

"It's working. The shades are coming," said Barthol, while I quickly scribed the portal spell. As I did, I pictured where Galin had been standing. I smiled as a portal crackled into existence in the tunnel.

"Be careful," I said as I started forward. "It's going to be a tight fit."

I slipped through the portal and into the hall near the thrones. From here, I looked across the great expanse of stone. The shades had gathered around the fire, ignoring us completely.

Barthol grunted quietly as he dropped through the portal. His bear fur jacket looked slightly singed.

I pointed at the arched door Galin had gone through—wooden, with sharp metal studs jutting out—and we hurried toward it.

When we reached it, I paused. I might be an Empress now, but I hadn't forgotten my years of assassin's training. What if all this was a trap? Galin, after all, hadn't looked quite himself. I glanced back around the cavernous tomb, at the shades bustling frantically around the fire. In the ancient stone walls, the blocks were dusty and chipped. I slid Levateinn into a gap between the stones, a plan already forming in my mind.

I reached for the door, ready to push it open, but before I could touch it, it swung towards me. At the first glimpse of his godlike face, I stepped back, like I'd been struck with an arrow.

"Galin?"

The sorcerer stood before me, arms crossed. His hair and eyes were now the color of the midnight sky, his chest tattooed with sharp black runes.

His expression was completely unreadable, like he was made of marble.

"Galin," I began again. "I got your message—"

I stopped short as a shadow moved in the passage behind him. The shimmer of a silk gown, blue skin, a pair of gray eyes that gleamed in the darkness. My heart leapt into my throat as the Goddess of the Dead stepped from a hidden alcove to join Galin.

Behind me, Barthol exhaled sharply.

For a long moment we all just stared at each other. Then Hela spoke in a husky voice, so quiet it was almost a whisper. "You must be Ali."

Dread shivered over my skin.

CHAPTER 7

ALI

ou got this, Ali.

"Not Ali." I straightened, clearing my throat. Adrenalin was filling my veins, making my body feel shaky. But I would compose myself. "I'm Empress of the Vanir."

Hela didn't reply, just stared at me—held my gaze too long, her gray eyes glittering. I stepped back, unnerved by the feeling that she was inspecting my soul. It took all my willpower not to look away.

If I were in her shoes I'd have been triumphant, exultant. I'd just caught my enemy in the middle of my stronghold, surrounded by my guards, with my most powerful warrior only feet away.

And what was Galin doing? Had he tricked me into coming here? Had he turned on me—or was he only pretending to be a shadowy weirdo?

Hela's expression remained placid, morose even. What was wrong with her? Were all the gods like this? Beautiful but dour?

Galin cocked his head, his expression a million miles

away. "Is that how you address the daughter of Loki, the Goddess of the Dead? The only living god?"

My breath left my lungs. I was starting to think perhaps Galin hadn't told me to come here at all. He certainly didn't look happy to see me.

What if Hela had summoned me?

My plan had failed. We'd been caught, and unless I could speak to Galin alone, I had no idea what he'd actually intended.

By his lack of expression, I guessed I had my answer to how he felt about me without the mating bond. He felt—nothing at all.

I tried to ignore the feeling of my heart shattering, so I could focus. That was what Swegde would tell me to do—push the emotions under the surface. I tore my gaze away from Galin, then dodged back from the doorway.

"Barthol, use your crystal," I shouted.

Except—Barthol didn't move. When I glanced at him, he seemed transfixed by Hela. That same expression that I'd seen in the tunnel was on his face again. I wanted to murder him. Absolutely murder him.

"You have something I want," said Hela in a low voice, her eyes fixed on me.

Definitely a trap, then. She'd lured me here—and like an idiot, I'd come running.

"And what would that be?" I said, feigning innocence.

"Give me the wand."

I shrugged, relieved at the one good decision I'd made—to hide it. "I don't have it."

Finally the goddess took her eyes off me. "Galin, darling. Search her."

Galin stepped in front of me. He towered over me, close enough that I could have run my fingers over the strange runes that covered the taught skin of his stomach. I could smell him too, sage and smoke. That part of him hadn't changed.

He reached for me. I went tense as his fingers brushed my shoulders, then traced along my arms.

Disappointment bloomed in my chest. He didn't look at me as he moved his hands along my ribs, down my hips. He ran his fingers over my legs, from my thighs down to my ankles. I stared at his queen as he did, and her gaze pierced me to the core. Gritting my teeth, I wished I'd never come here.

After confirming the wand wasn't hidden under my leather pants, Galin straightened. "She doesn't have it."

Hela took a step closer. "Where is my wand, Empress?"

"Back in Vanaheim. I couldn't risk bringing it with me."

Galin still loomed over me. "That's impossible, she couldn't have gotten here without it."

Anger roiled in my mind. *Screw you, Galin. Shadowy prick.*

And this was why I'd needed to sever the mating bond. Because without it? He didn't care for me at all. He'd written the letter to trap me here. That was all.

"I had one of the seidr send me here," I said sharply. "I didn't use the wand."

Galin's body was eerily still, shadows curling from him. "One cannot create a portal to a place they haven't visited. You and I are the only mortals to have toured this realm in thousands of years. The seidr did not send you here."

My fingers tightened into fists. Had I actually thought we might have something without the mating bond? Absolute idiocy.

"I described the realm in great detail."

A muscle twitched in his jaw. "The Night Elf lies. It's close by."

But Hela didn't appear to be listening to Galin. Instead she was looking past me.

She was staring at Barthol.

"Who is *he*?" Her voice was a quiet murmur.

He gazed at her with wonder. "I am Barthol Volundar, the Empress's brother."

Gods, what was Barthol doing? Telling Hela he was my brother gave her leverage over me. This was a basic assassin no-no.

"Yes, her brother," Hela murmured, gliding towards him, her silk robe shimmering. "And what brings *you* to my kingdom?"

"Well," Barthol stammered, "I was looking after Ali."

She arched an eyebrow. "You mean the Empress of the Vanir?"

"Err, yes."

"I see." Hela's voice was buttery smooth. "And does that mean you know where the wand is?"

Barthol stared at the goddess like he'd been hypnotized. It didn't help that the sheerness of the silk hid absolutely nothing.

"I don't ... I haven't ..." Barthol's throat bobbed.

"Why don't you just tell me the last time you saw the wand?" whispered Hela, catching Barthol's chin in her long fingers.

Barthol had gone completely rigid, his eyes fixed on Hela's. He opened his mouth, but no sound came out.

"Silly boy," said Hela. "You don't need to be scared of me."

"I'm not scared of you," he whispered.

The death stare I was giving him had no effect, since he wasn't looking at me.

"Then tell me where the wand is," she purred.

"It's ..." Barthol stammered again. Hela leaned closer, drawing a finger along the edge of his jaw.

I glanced to Galin. He was watching Hela intently. This was my chance.

Leaping past him, I snatched Levateinn from the crevice in the stone. Before Galin could stop me, I leveled the wand at Hela.

"Step away from my brother, goddess."

The goddess turned to look at me. Her movements were slow, like a reptile just warming up after a cold night, her dark eyes expressionless. Was it possible she didn't actually care about the wand?

She held out her hand. "Give it to me. It is mine."

Her body went preternaturally still, and it took all my willpower not to look away. A cold dread was spilling through me. My tongue felt heavy in my mouth, and my jaw didn't want to open. Still, I somehow managed to say, "No."

If the goddess was surprised to hear that, her expression didn't show it. As she studied me with her dark eyes, I felt a deep foreboding. A clammy chill spread over my skin, and my heart seemed to beat more slowly in my chest.

It had to be magic. Whatever she had done to Barthol, she was doing to me now. A death spell?

"Is this the wand, Galin?"

"Yes, Goddess."

"Please bring it to me."

Galin stepped forward, ready to take the wand. With an iron will, I forced myself to step back.

"You cannot run, Empress," Hela hissed.

"Barthol," I gasped. "Help me."

Across from me, Barthol remained focused on the goddess. He took a step towards her. Slowly his arms spread open. Then, grinning like an idiot, he wrapped the goddess in one of his massive bear hugs.

Galin moved for me then, but the goddess's gaze had shifted from me. Free of her magic, I dove hard to the side, evading him with a roll to the ground.

As I leapt to my feet, I dodged him again, farther away

this time. Shifting out of Galin's reach, I cast a portal spell with a crackle of electric magic.

The portal opened a foot to my right, no more than eight inches wide—a direct conduit between Hela's tomb and my chambers in the Vanir temple.

Static electricity crackled round my wrist as I shoved the wand through.

"Get any closer and I'll drop it," I shouted.

Galin went still—five feet away from me. Behind him, Barthol still hugged Hela. What in gods' name was he doing?

"If you drop the wand, you'll be trapped here." A sharp edge undercut Galin's voice.

"Do you really think I'm that stupid?" I shot him a bitter smile. "I've got my vergr crystal back in Vanaheim. I can leave at any time—wand or no wand."

For the first time since we'd been talking, I saw an emotion on Galin's face: worry.

"Didn't anticipate that, did you?" My smile deepened. "So here's the plan. You're going to take a little vacation with Barthol and me. I'll return you when the draugr are actually trapped in Hel once more. Then you can have your queen back."

Hela's monotone voice cut in, "And what do I get in exchange?"

"This isn't a negotiation." I kept my eyes on Galin as I spoke, in case he made a move for me.

"But I think it is," said Hela coolly.

"You have nothing to negotiate with," I shot back.

"But I do."

I peeked at Hela out of the corner of my eye. She'd extracted herself from Barthol's embrace. Now he stood beside her, staring at her again with puppy-dog eyes.

She stroked his cheek, and something like panic started to steal my breath.

"Barthol!" I shouted. "Use your crystal."

Barthol didn't move, didn't even seem to hear me. He continued to gaze rapturously at Hela.

Bringing him here was the worst mistake I'd made in a long time.

"Barthol," I shouted again, "your crystal."

"Barthol," crooned Hela. "I am the Goddess of the Dead. You love me."

Barthol's eyes widened, as if this were the first time he'd heard that. "You are the Goddess of the Dead," he intoned.

"Kneel before me," said Hela.

"Barthol! Don't listen to her!" I was practically screaming. But if Barthol heard me, he didn't acknowledge it. Slowly he knelt in front of Hela, his eyes locked on hers.

"Draw your sword," she purred.

Barthol did as he was commanded.

I screamed at him, but he continued to ignore me.

Hela smiled, her eyes ice cold. "Now, press it against your neck."

He pressed the blade against his own neck, and nausea rose in my gut.

"So you see," said Hela, turning to look at me again. "I *do* have something to negotiate with."

Terror wound through me. Just like the Nokk had done to Galin, Barthol was completely mind controlled.

"Barthol," I shouted again, vainly hoping to get through to him. "Use your crystal."

"Give me the wand." Hela held out her hand. "And I will release your brother."

I looked to Barthol, my heart slamming against my ribs. I had to make a choice.

I could let Hela kill him, or I could give up the wand. But if I left the wand, then I had no way to get back to Hel.

My people—all elves—would die at the hands and teeth of the draugr. I'd have failed completely as Empress.

It might take months, or years, but I knew in my bones we'd be overrun. I could save Barthol now, but in the end? He'd die with the rest of us.

But maybe there was another way—it was just one that involved sacrificing the wand, and I would be putting all my trust in Galin. What other choice did I have?

I pulled the wand from the portal. "Release him, and you can have it."

Hela nodded, her eyes half closed, expression stony.

"Get me the wand, my dark king," she said to Galin.

Galin crossed to me, but as he reached for the wand, I threw it behind Hela, watching as she turned to look at it. Then I lunged forward, and wrapped my arms around Galin.

All it took was one word to connect us to the vergr stone —and I just had to pray that my brother would come to his senses and follow.

Light flashed, and Galin and I disappeared.

CHAPTER 8

ALI

For a moment, my eyes blazed with violet light. Then, the light faded, and I found myself in my quarters again, my arms wrapped around Galin's chiseled chest. I forced myself to step back.

"You can stay away from me." My voice sounded like ice. "You're only here because I needed a sorcerer to stop the draugr. And now, if Barthol doesn't return, you will be collateral. When we're done, I will trade you for my brother. Clearly, you belong in Hel."

"Is that right?" he said tonelessly.

Anger still vibrated through me, and I glanced at the stones sitting on a shelf by an open window. They glimmered faintly, casting violet light over the clean white walls, and the gauzy drapes that floated in the breeze. One was mine, the other Barthol's. His crystal was right where he'd left it.

We'd lost the wand, but all Barthol had to do was say the word.

I closed my eyes, uttering a silent prayer. *Please say the word. Please give him back to me.*

But who was I praying to? Only one god walked the nine

realms, and she was the living nightmare who'd trapped my brother.

I pulled his crystal from the shelf, clutching it as I willed him to appear. My chest grew tighter, dread sliding through my blood.

A minute passed, then another, but there was no sign of my brother. *Dammit Barthol. Just say the word.*

I felt Galin's warmth near me, and smelled his scent of wood smoke and sage. I opened my eyes to see those midnight eyes on me.

He peered down at me, faintly curious. "He won't be coming. Hela's persuasive powers are unparalleled. I've only recently started to learn to resist them."

A million objections screamed in my mind, but through them all, a clear and quiet voice told me that I would find a way to get Barthol back. There was simply no question—I was not going to leave him there with the Goddess of the Dead.

Galin had tricked me, and now, my brother had paid the price.

"Your letter called us there," I hissed. "Nice little trap you and your queen set for me. And this is why I had to sever the mating bond—to find out that deep down under that sexy exterior, you're a monster. Now I know the truth."

He flinched, almost imperceptibly. The runes inked on his chest shimmered ominously. His expression was as grim as the shadowy magic that drifted around him. "And if you hadn't severed the ties, I might never have realized I was entranced by a selfish wretch. I'd be thankful, except I no longer feel anything at all."

Fury ignited in me, and the words rang in my mind. "Nothing?"

"Certainly not desire."

I tried to see through my haze of anger to focus. "Same

with me," I lied. But I was losing focus now, and there were more important things to discuss. "Wait. What do you mean her persuasive powers are unparalleled?"

"Hela's magic is invasive. It descends on your mind like a shroud. Once she sinks her death magic into you, it's not easy to think on your own."

My throat tightened. "Okay. Wait. Did she force you to be her lover against your will? Is that how you ended up as her consort?"

The breeze toyed with his hair. "No."

Nausea rose in my gut, and I glared at him, reminding myself that it was none of my business. "Okay. Never mind. Why did you tell her that Barthol was my brother, giving her leverage over me?"

"You don't need to be a goddess to see how alike you and Barthol are. She knew. She tests people. It's what she does."

I inhaled deeply. "And when you tried to take the wand from me," I said. "Was that her influence?"

"I wasn't trying to take the wand from you."

I blinked. "Yeah, you were. I was there."

"If I wanted to take the wand from you, I would have taken it. If I didn't want to leave Hel with you, I would not be here now. You're an assassin of the highest order, but your raw physical strength is no match for mine. I told her where the wand was because she knew it was there. It's Loki's wand —her father's wand, connected to her magic. Even I could feel its power. She was testing you, testing me. Trying to see what we would do. She wanted to see if I still felt anything for you. I had to play along, or she would have just killed you. It would have been better if you hadn't showed up exactly when she was there."

Shadows darkened the air around him. "And it would have been better if you hadn't brought your brother. The bottom line is—Barthol won't be breaking out. But having me here is leverage. You were right about that much, she wants me in Hel."

Horror washed over me as I thought of what my brother was being subjected to. I caught myself on the edge of the table as the room seemed to spin. "I have to get him out."

"I will return to the goddess as her consort, and you will get your brother back. As you said, I belong in Hel."

I arched an eyebrow. "If you're so loyal to this goddess, then why are you defying her?"

"I want to stop the draugr hordes from destroying the world. I was the one who raised her. It's my responsibility to fix this. And when I return, you'll get Barthol back." He was offering to save my brother, but an edge of steel undercut his voice. "That is what you want, right?"

"None of this is really what I wanted." I started pacing, my mind still whirling with panic. "Will Hela hurt him?"

"No, not physically at least."

I frowned. "That's not exactly reassuring."

A knock sounded on my door.

"Yes?" I asked.

"Empress, it's Swegde," he called through the door.

"You may enter."

The door swung open, and Swegde's eyebrows crept up when he saw Galin. "You returned with the sorcerer." His eyes moved from Galin, back to me, then to the rest of the room. "Where is Barthol?"

"In Hel," said Galin.

Swegde's eyes widened, and I saw on his face the horror I'd felt only moments earlier. "Dead?"

"No, he's alive," I said quickly. "Hela took him as collateral —to insure Galin's safe return." It wasn't exactly the truth, but I didn't want Swegde freaking out.

Swegde narrowed his eyes at Galin. "You will return in exchange for Barthol?"

"Yes. There is little for me here, anyway."

Disappointment slid through me.

A muscle in Swegde's jaw worked. As much as I believed in Galin, he did not. "The council is waiting for you," he said at last.

* * *

Seated at the council table were Bo, Lynheid, Harald, and Sigre. Their eyes widened as they took in Galin—and the fierce-looking tattoos that slid over his muscles. From a chandelier above us, candlelight wavered, shadows moving back and forth over the room.

"He's here." Lynheid stood. "But where is Barthol?"

"He remains in Hel as Hela's prisoner. We will get him back," I said. "Don't worry."

Harald's face had gone pale, muscles rigid. With a scrape of steel he drew his sword, lip curled. "I am Harald, Prince of Midgard. As ruler of the High Elves, I place you under arrest."

Galin stared at him, hardly moving. "On what charges?"

"You committed the most serious of crimes: regicide, patricide, fratricide. You killed King Gorm, and you pushed your brother to his death. Do you dispute this?"

"No."

"Then you will submit?" Harald stalked towards Galin.

"No."

That was his whole defense? During his time in Hel, Galin had become even more reticent than usual. He hardly spoke more than he had when he'd been a lich.

I sighed. "Put your sword away, Harald."

Ignoring me, Harald readied his sword. He stood five feet from Galin, close enough to strike.

Galin had gone still as stone, his black eyes locked on Harald.

Harald lunged. I shouted for him to stop, but it was too late. He drove his blade towards Galin's chest, but just as the sword plunged into the sorcerer, Galin whispered a spell.

Darkness filled the room, the candles snuffing out at once.

There was a crash, and Harald swore. Then, the candles flickered to life again, bathing the room in warm light.

I stared. Where Galin had been, there were only wisps of black smoke. He'd completely disappeared. Harald's sword was lodged in the oak table. Now armed with only a dagger, the prince slashed at the empty air.

"Where is he?" he shouted, his face red.

"Here." Galin reappeared beside him. Harald spun, but not before Galin's fist slammed into his jaw. Harald crumpled to the floor, and his knife spun across the stone.

My muscles tensed; I was quickly losing control of this situation. "May I remind you—"

My lecture was drowned out by a shriek from Sigre as she yanked the hair pin from her platinum hair. Hefting it like a throwing knife, she flung it at Galin. This time the blade found its mark. The hairpin quivered in Galin's shoulder.

Galin yanked it out and stared at it. "Poisoned with eitr?"

"Now you die," said Sigre, her eyes wild. "As you should."

"I am the King of the Hel. Eitr cannot hurt me." His deep voice boomed over the room. "You'll need more than that to keep me down."

"You died twice," said Sigre. "You no longer have the right to rule the High Elves. You are an abomination, and you will not have our throne."

"Is that what this is about?" Galin's voice was ice. "You're concerned about who sits on the High Elf throne?"

"You wish to steal it back," said Sigre, though she now sounded less sure of herself. "You abdicated the throne when you fell into the Well of Wyrd. The rightful claim now lies with the house of Scylfing."

"The Scylfings?" Galin spat. "Is that who rules the High Elves now?"

She flicked her blonde hair over her shoulder. "Yes."

"Then they deserve you."

Sigre stared, caught completely off guard. "What?"

Galin straightened. "The High Elves chose poorly."

At Galin's feet, Prince Harald stirred. "Is the abomination dead?"

"Unfortunately for you, I am very much alive." Galin peered down at him. "Do not try to kill me again. Understood?"

The prince made a groaning noise.

"I'll take that as a yes."

Sigre glared at Galin, but she didn't speak.

"Are you quite finished?" I asked. "We are, after all, here to discuss the draugr."

Galin cut me a sharp look. "Assuming there are no more attempts on my life."

"Then let us discuss our plans. You're working against your lovely queen in secret." I pinned him with my gaze. "Why, exactly?"

His dark eyes locked on mine. "As I said privately, I was the one who raised the goddess from the dead. I will not allow the draugr to overrun the realms that I love. I am and always will be a protector of Midgard and the nine realms from the forces of darkness, as I was before Ragnarok. Even if it means defying a goddess."

I breathed out, relieved to learn he really wasn't blindingly loyal to the goddess. "Okay. So as a protector of the nine realms, now would be a great time to fulfill your end of the bargain." I bit my lip. "But if you return to Hel after defying her, what will she do to you?"

"Don't worry about me. I will find a way out." The shadows drifting around Galin thickened. "Right now, our goal is to defeat the draugr. Let's stay focused on that."

Swegde stepped forward. "All right, sorcerer, then it's time you started building a wall to keep them out."

Galin shook his head. "That won't work."

"Why not?" Bo glared at Galin from his place at the table. "You seemed to have no trouble keeping my people imprisoned for a thousand years."

"Draugr are not elves. And besides, Hela has closed the gates to Hel."

My stomach flipped. "She *what*?"

"She's shut the gate in the iron wall," said Galin. "No souls may enter. This is why the dead now roam the lands of the living."

"But, why?" I asked.

"Because she wants to take over the nine realms. She wants to unleash the draugr and shades and rule over a world of the dead. Closing the gates to Hel is her first step. But she plans total domination of all nine realms."

I glanced at the writhing tattoos on his chest. "If she can control you, what will stop her from bringing you back to Hel right now? She has the wand, and once she has you, she can just break free from Hel with your help. And she can mind control you or whatever to do it."

He shook his head. "Fortunately, her persuasive powers don't work from this far. And the runes around the iron walls of Hel were inscribed by the gods. They will stop her from breaking out—even with me there. Even with the wand. But she is searching for a way out."

A terrible understanding dawned on me. "So if we kill the draugr …"

"They will not disappear," said Galin grimly. "And in a war, their numbers will only grow, no matter what you do. The more elves die, the more draugr we have on earth. That's what it means that the Gates of Hel are closed."

"So what can we do?" asked Bo.

Galin cocked his head. "You can start by not dying."

Frustration simmered. "How do you plan to help, then? Can you just spit it out, Galin, so we can get Barthol back?"

Galin's expression softened. "We need to visit Mimisbrunnr."

I shook my head. "I don't know what that is."

Candlelight danced in Galin's eyes. "When Odin was young, before he became the King of Asgard and leader of the gods, he wished to learn all that there was to know. So he traveled to Mimisbrunnr, the Well of Knowledge. Mimir, the well keeper, allowed him to drink from the waters, but only if he gave up his eye. Odin immediately drew a knife and carved out his right eye. This is how he learned more than any man could learn in a thousand lifetimes. This is how he learned of the runes and the rules of magic. This is how he was able to convince the gods to name him as their leader."

"I know the story of Odin's sacrifice," interrupted Bo. "What is the plan?"

"Like Odin, I will drink from Mimisbrunnr. The waters of the well will show me how to defeat the draugr."

"This is your plan?" I asked. "Drink from a magic well?" Clearly, I was still feeling salty with Galin.

His dark gaze rooted me in place, taking me apart. "You wanted me to help because of my knowledge of sorcery. And now it seems you don't trust that same knowledge. Why?"

Because you are breaking my heart.

"Because you're consort to the person who caused all this, and clearly she has influence over you," I said quietly. "But I suppose we don't have a lot of options. How do we get there?"

"Mimisbrunnr is somewhere in Asgard. Unfortunately, I never visited the home of the gods."

"So no portal then?" I said.

Galin shook his head. "We'll have to go the old way. Over the Bifrost bridge."

Swegde looked confused. "The Bifrost was destroyed during Ragnarok."

Galin shook his head. "For the gods it was, but we're elves. I believe it will still support my weight. I will go alone."

I stared at him, certain there was something he wasn't telling me. Something important, and I didn't like it. What if he was still working for Hela?

"No, you won't go alone," I said. "This is supposed to be a joint effort. We'll join you."

Shadows seeped into the air around him. "It won't work. The bridge would never hold that many people. And a large number is more likely to slow us down. You just said you trusted me to solve this problem, didn't you?"

"I'll go with you then," I barked. As the others began to object, I held up a hand. "That's final."

"Very well," said Galin. "Ali—the Empress—and I will travel to Jotunfjell. The top of Mount Steton is where we find the Bifrost."

Wonderful. It seemed I would be spending some time with my ex—after he'd moved on.

CHAPTER 9

GALIN

Across the room from me, Ali slowly nodded. "Okay. Whatever it takes. We'll leave in the morning. Swegde, can you organize hiking equipment?"

Swegde nodded, and my gaze slid back to Ali. I studied her—silver hair pulled up in a ponytail, eyes slightly narrowed. Her outfit was familiar assassin's garb: leather pants and a black jacket that fit her curves perfectly. Everything was splattered with mud, but she didn't seem to care. She may have only been Empress for a month, but already she was accustomed to being listened to. She looked strong, powerful. More confident, more poised than I remembered.

The members of the council listened carefully when she spoke, even the murderous twins. I would have to ask her how they'd been chosen to represent the High Elves; their family was known for castrating their enemies. Still, even with Harald and Sigre in her council, Ali was clearly in charge, a natural leader.

And in her new role, she had made it quite clear that she'd easily moved on from me.

And this is why I had to sever the mating bond—to find out that deep down under that sexy exterior, you're still a monster.

I smiled grimly. At least she'd called me sexy.

It didn't matter what she said. With the mating bond cut, anything I'd felt had withered away like vines in the frost.

"Galin," she said. "We need to talk. In private. Will you walk with me back to my room?"

I nodded and followed her into the hallway. As we started walking, she glanced at my chest. No—she was staring.

"So when are you going to put on a shirt?" she asked. "It's distracting."

A smile ghosted over my lips. "Distracting? Why would that be? Is it the sexy exterior that's a problem?"

Her cheeks reddened. "No. As we have *both* agreed, neither of us feel anything for each other. Right? Anything that happened before was just magic. Now you might as well be ..." She gestured at a candle in a sconce. "You're like that candle. That is how much emotion I feel."

"Right, we feel nothing at all. And yet you seem flustered," I murmured.

"Did you get a bit of an ego as King of the Dead, or did I just never notice how bad it was before?"

"I was just repeating your phrase," I purred. "Sexy exterior. Your words."

She shook her head, a strand of silver falling before her eyes. "I meant sexy in an objective way. Other people would say you are sexy, probably. Simple-minded people. What I meant was that your bare chest is distracting because of the runes. They move in a distracting way."

"The runes are a gift from the goddess. A shirt would disturb them."

Her jaw tightened, and anger shone in her eyes when she looked at me. Jealousy? "A gift. How *nice* of her. What a lovely woman. Are they what allowed you to disappear?"

"With them inked on my skin I can move from one place

to another without calling a portal. But they bind me to Hela, as well."

Ali nodded, her lips pressed into a thin line. "Like branding an animal. You're her beast of burden. It's quite the relationship you two have."

Irritation sparked. So *this* was what she was like without the mating bond.

An absolute nightmare.

"Why exactly did you ask me to speak to you in private? Was it to talk about my chest, or to insult me? I could do without either. Considering neither of us feel a thing for each other, perhaps our time could be better spent getting ready for the journey."

"No." She shot me another nervous look, her face flushed. "I think we might have gotten off to a bad start. If we are going to go off together, we should probably be on better terms."

"And how do you propose to make that happen?"

She lifted her eyebrows hopefully. "Are you hungry?"

We'd reached the door to her quarters. I frowned, unused to feeling anything at all. But I *did* feel a hollowness in my stomach. Hunger. "Famished."

Ali led me inside. When I was in her quarters before, my senses had been adjusting to Vanaheim, the sunlight, the scent of living things. I hadn't really looked around me.

"This is the old Emperor's chambers," I said.

My memories stirred. The old Emperor had attacked Ali, tried to have his way with her. She killed him, but it was close. I couldn't imagine why she'd want to stay in the same rooms where he once lived.

"Yes," said Ali. "All Vanir Emperors have lived in these quarters. Hundreds, I've been told. Swegde said there was no other option."

I gritted my teeth, increasingly certain I didn't like Swegde.

But as I looked around, I saw that Ali had been busy decorating. She'd brought in more plants, and some large crystals that I assumed must have been from the Shadow Caverns.

She'd even hung a painting of a goat on the wall—one that appeared to be standing on top of a large purple mushroom. I looked closer. Was it drinking a beer?

Ali pointed at it. "That's Jeremy the Alcoholic Goat. Barthol painted it for me. You see? The world cannot live without his talent."

She was making a joke, but I could hear the worry in her voice. "He will be fine. Hela wants me to return. As long as I go back to my place as King of the Dead, I don't think she'll hurt him."

I surveyed the rest of the room. I recognized the double doors that led to the pool. Nearby was a shelf arranged with a large collection of LPs and a small record player.

In the dark ashes of my chest, something stirred. "You have a whole music collection?"

"Yes," said Ali. "Okay, it might be indulgent, but they asked me what I wanted for my room. And I wanted music from Midgard. I haven't had a chance to see what they chose for me yet."

She crossed over to the records. When her arm brushed against mine—for just a moment—I thought I felt a quickening of my heart. I watched as she pulled out an album I hadn't seen in a thousand years. She stared at the cover.

"What is this?" she murmured. "All these men in strange costumes with flowers. It's pretty."

Ali pulled the record out and dropped it onto the player. Wonderful music filled the air—songs from a time long ago. As it played, she walked to the door. Under the song, I heard her speaking to a servant outside, ordering dinner for us both.

She crossed back into the room with an uncertain smile on her face. Once my mate, now we just felt awkward around each other. She bit her lip. "I really like the tune, but the lyrics don't make any sense. Is it about stars?"

"It's called 'Lucy in the Sky with Diamonds.' It's short for LSD. A hallucinogenic drug from the world of man."

"Oh!" said Ali. "Like berserker mushrooms, or fairy wine."

Now it was my turn to be confused. "Fairy wine?"

"You haven't heard of fairy wine? I thought you were a famous sorcerer."

"I never claimed to be omniscient. Just to have a sexy exterior. That's my main claim to fame."

She glowered at me, which delighted me. "Well, fairy wine is wine that fairies drink. It makes you lose your inhibitions, but it can be an aphrodisiac. If you weren't dead inside you'd have to be careful. But as it is, I don't think you'd need to worry."

I quirked an eyebrow. "Have you tried it?"

"Oh no," said Ali, a little too quickly. "Barthol drank some at the last feast. He went crazy, but fortunately not in an aphrodisiac way, or I would have vomited. He just ran around in his cave bear jacket while shouting that he was the Goat King." She folded her arms. "I'm sure it's not as fun as being King of Hel."

"Fun means nothing to me anymore." I wasn't lying. Ever since the severing of the mating bond, I felt as though I'd been hollowed out, emptied of desire, a husk of my former self. The worst part was, I could remember those feelings, the unquenchable thirst, the burning *need* for my mate. But now that was gone. Without the fate the Norns had written for me, I was unmoored.

I could recognize Ali's sublime beauty, but inside my

chest it was as if someone had poured water on a fire—nothing but wet ashes remained.

So I would return to Hel—long enough to get her brother back. But then I would find a way to break free. I would not remain consort of Hela for long.

And that was the other reason I needed to get to Mimisbrunnr. The well's waters would reveal my new fate. I would be made whole again, with a shining path before me.

I would feel again, truly live again.

A knock sounded at the door, and a moment later a guard wheeled in a cart piled with food. He rolled it over to the window, and began sliding dishes onto a table there, along with a platter of various cheeses, pickled vegetables, and cured meats. "There is charcuterie, a fresh loaf of sourdough, a watercress salad with pine nuts, and a roast chicken with sage." He lifted a silver cloche to reveal a steaming chicken.

I took a seat across from Ali. After a month in Hel eating gruel, even my dead heart could recognize how delicious the food smelled.

The servant pulled a bottle from the tray. "This is a local varietal, similar to Syrah. Jammy, with a hint of blackberries." He opened the wine, then poured glasses for Ali and me.

I took a sip. The flavor exploded across my palette, and I almost felt a hint of enjoyment before the sensation faded again.

Ali tried hers. "This is delicious."

The servant smiled. "I'm very glad you enjoy it, Empress."

As he left, Ali grinned. "The Vanir are all really into food. I've come a long way from mushroom soup."

I started with the slightly tart watercress salad, then the rich, earthy chicken.

And yet, only when I had a new fate would I truly enjoy food again.

I glanced at Ali as I sipped my wine, feeling a million

miles away from her still—no longer my mate, the wild Night Elf. She was now Empress of the Vanir.

She studied me with silver eyes. How long would it be until someone tried to make this beauty his wife?

Darkness sank into my bones.

I rose from the table. "I'm afraid I'm not hungry after all."

She frowned. "Right. Dead inside."

"But I will meet you in the morning, Ali. We will do fine as traveling companions."

I left the room, shadows spreading through my chest.

CHAPTER 10

ALI

We'd been hiking for hours in complete silence. I wanted to sit, drink some water from the canteen on my hip, maybe take in the view. But some kind of stupid pride made me reluctant to admit I was tired. Or maybe a competitiveness with the Goddess of the Dead. She'd never have tired legs.

So as much as my legs burned, I pushed on. *Pain,* I reminded myself, *is something I can handle.* I looked at my missing finger. It wasn't long ago that I'd cauterized it on a hot stove. A walk through fields? I could handle that.

And yet I wasn't sure what was more painful—my tired muscles, or the total silence from Galin. Or the knowledge that he'd been a willing consort of Hela.

What an idiot I'd been to think he'd still like me after I severed the mating bond. *Stupid, stupid Ali.*

At least the scenery was gorgeous.

We'd started in Jotunfjell's boreal forest of spruce and Scots pine, where squirrels and birds skittered among the branches. As we gained elevation, we crossed into beautiful alpine meadows. Here, bees and butterflies flew among the grasses dappled with yellow wildflowers. Little rodents perched on top of boulders, squeaking loudly if we got too close. Galin told me they were called lemmings.

Above us, in the bluebird-blue sky, soared massive eagles.

Being aboveground still felt glorious. It would never get old.

We pressed on, hiking towards the looming edifice of Mount Steton. The sides of the granite slope were bare rock, which steepened until they reached a narrow peak with a flat top, like the end of a dagger that had been snapped off. I had no idea how we were going to climb the thing, but Galin was confident we could do it.

Still there was no sign of the Bifrost bridge. It was supposed to extend from the peak of Mount Steton all the way to Asgard, but as far as I could see there was nothing up there but empty air.

All day, Galin had been brooding and taciturn, still refusing to put on a shirt.

"Aren't you cold?" I asked.

"No," he said quietly. "The magic of Hel keeps me warm."

"What exactly does Hela's magic do? I mean apart from the whole disappearing and reappearing thing."

"It strengthens me. She's imbued the runes with her power. As long as I wear them, I can draw upon her strength."

"I see," I said slowly. "So they're sort of like a wand that's been tattooed onto your skin."

"Or I'm like a branded beast, as you said."

I swallowed hard. "Are you worried about what she will do after you return to Hel? You're ruining her plans right now."

"I will find a way to survive, Ali. I always have. Even if it meant being dead for a thousand years. I'm still here."

It wasn't as reassuring as I would have hoped.

We walked in silence again, the trail twisting along the edge of a meadow before ducking into a grove of aspens. As we followed the path between the spindly trees, a gentle gust of wind rustled the leaves, spinning them like the wings of a thousand butterflies. From there, we continued on to a rocky talus slope. More of the lemmings squeaked at us.

I glanced at Galin again, still bothered by the runes. "Why can't you just use your own magic to keep you warm?"

"Well, when I had Levateinn I would scribe the runes in the right order, and then something magical would happen, like a portal or a gout of fire. Scribing the runes, plus having the wand made the magic happen. Now I don't need the wand—I have Loki's magic through his daughter."

"What's the source? A god's soul?"

The wind toyed with his dark hair. "We all have some magic. You have magic right now. In fact, you have enough magic in your body to do all the things you could do when you had Levateinn."

"What?"

A smile ghosted over his beautiful lips. "Magic is innate. You just need to learn to draw upon it."

"Whoa," I whispered. Was it really possible that I could do magic without Levateinn?

I stopped and extended my index finger, as I'd seen Galin do a hundred times before. Quickly I scribed the runes for the fire spell.

Nothing happened.

Galin was watching me, curiosity gleaming in his eyes. "Your dexterity is excellent, but casting a spell is more than just scribing the runes. You have to put *yourself* into it. The magic comes from your emotions. For fire magic, you need to feel rage. Scribing the runes transforms that emotion into tangible fire. Did you feel angry when you were scribing?"

"No. Just …" Tired, which I didn't want to admit.

Galin nodded. "Ok, watch me."

He raised his right hand, his brow furrowed with concentration, then effortlessly traced the fire runes.

An instant later, a three-foot flame burst from the air ten feet in front of him. It guttered for a second in the alpine wind, before he extinguished it with a flick of his wrist.

"But without emotions, I must use Hela's magic. Why don't you try scribing the fire spell again? This time think of something that makes you angry. A dangerously sexy egomaniacal monster, perhaps."

Frowning at him, I raised my right hand. Again I scribed the runes. This time, as I spoke them out loud, I thought of Hela. First she'd taken Galin. Then she'd taken Barthol. My poor brother was trapped in Hel, probably imprisoned in some dank dungeon surrounded by shades.

The image of Hela striding naked from her bathroom intruded on my consciousness. Of course he'd been her consort of his own free will. What man could resist a goddess?

Sadness tightened my throat, and my concentration flagged.

"Crap," I said, dropping my arm.

"It's more difficult than it looks, isn't it? It took me more than a year before I could cast my first fire spell. I'm not sure if you noticed, but the air shimmered with a little heat. The issue is that you lost focus. You need to hold the rage, all the way until the spell is complete. You know how you call Skalei?"

"Yes," I said, not understanding how my shadow blade had anything to do with scribing the fire spell.

"Well, you believe Skalei will come any time you call her, right? The dagger is part of you."

"Yes ..." The very thought of Skalei not coming for me

was terrifying. She was always there for me, razor sharp protection at my literal fingertips. I'd nearly lost my mind in the Audr Prison Mine when she was taken from me.

"Magic's the same way. You have to believe that it will work, that it's part of you. Magic comes from the strength of your feelings. And that is why I need Hela's runes."

I stared at him. "You are alive again. You are no longer a lich. You should be able to feel. I don't understand what happened to you."

"You did." He turned, walking away from me again.

The words stole my breath. *Gods alive.*

I hurried to keep up with him. "What do you mean?"

"My fate was written by the Norns. Without it, I am only half alive. It's not important. I was going to tell you about Hela's magic."

"Right." I was starting to hate the subject of Hela.

"The gods don't have souls," he said. "At least not in the mortal sense. Instead their magic comes from their worshipers. Ancient Midgard had a story called *Peter Pan*. There's a fairy named Tinker Bell. It was written by a human, so the magic is totally made up, but there's a famous line where it's explained that if a child says they don't believe in fairies then somewhere a fairy falls down dead. Basically fairies exist only because children believe in them. The gods are the same. Because we all believe in them, they have power."

I grimaced. "Despite the dead fairies in that book, it still sounds more cheerful than the stories the Night Elves tell their kids. There is a monster called Enlil who will eat your toes off if you don't trim your fingernails, and a witch who'll bake you alive if you don't listen to your parents. Anyway, so if I want to do magic, I just have to learn to feel incandescently angry at a moment's notice?"

"For the fire spell, yes. Other spells require different emotions. The spell for light requires happiness, and the portal spell requires you to feel love."

Wonderful. "Okay, well I will work on that." My tone had gone frosty, and I wondered what kind of magic quiet rage and a searing sense of betrayal could create.

Probably not anything good.

And yet, I wanted to try again.

I turned, staring out over the vista. Spread before me were thickly forested foothills, which tumbled down to the distant plains of Vanaheim. "Okay. Let me give this another shot."

"I'll help." Galin stepped behind me. "Try the fire spell again, but this time just incant the words. I'll take care of the scribing."

He took hold of my hands. I stared at his thumbs and forefingers, effortlessly encircling my wrists. High Elves were enormous. His powerful forearms were close to, but not quite touching mine.

Gently he lifted my arms. I could smell him now, wood smoke and sage. Familiar but distant, like something from a dream.

Black vapor from the runes on his chest drifted over my shoulders. *Hela's magic.*

"You need to focus," whispered Galin. "What makes you angry?"

What had he said to me? That he was glad I'd severed the ties with him so he didn't end up with a selfish wretch?

That should do it.

And then there was Hela, who had branded Galin and stolen Barthol.

"Concentrate," Galin whispered.

The problem was, when I thought of Hela, or of Galin's

dismissal of me, a different emotion started to seep in: sadness.

I needed to think of something else.

So as I closed my eyes, I remembered how I'd been full of rage when I was imprisoned in the Audr Mine. Back then, I was thinking of all the ways I could hurt Galin—the High Elf prince who I thought had betrayed me. I wanted him dead.

But he hadn't betrayed me, had he? It had all been a trick played on me by Revna and Gorm, with forged letters.

All the time I'd been suffering in the mine, Galin had been trapped in the Citadel, desperately trying to save me.

Galin swung my hands through the shapes of the runes as I tried to remember the words to the spell. I breathed in, as if I might fill my lungs with rage, but instead I smelled Galin again. Warmth from his body radiated over me. Once, I'd been curled up in his arms.

That wood smoke was so distinctive. Did he smell like that naturally?

"Are you focused?" he purred.

"Yes," I said, too quickly. I turned to face him. "I was just thinking of the time Barthol ate sixty-three portobello mushrooms on a dare and threw up all over our house. I was livid. It's not working, though."

Galin stared at me, the icy breeze rippling over us.

"Let me try without you for a moment."

Turning from him, I hurried up the trail, without looking back.

That had been disorienting. I felt something for him, and he'd made it clear that nothing was returned.

It was better this way, I reminded myself. I had a kingdom to rule.

I just needed Galin's help for this final task. Once the draugr were sent back to Hel, I could focus on my people.

The Norn had been clear—an Empress's duty, first and fore-most, was to her people.

And if I needed to learn magic, I could figure it out on my own.

So why did I still feel like my heart was breaking?

CHAPTER 11

GALIN

I walked behind Ali. The sun stained the sky with peach, gold, and violet—a riot of warmth spreading over the blue-gray crags around us. Hours ago, we'd left the forest, and we now climbed a steep slope of football-sized boulders.

Even in the gathering darkness, I had no trouble seeing the massive headwall of Mount Steton. It rose up like the side of the Citadel—a sheer face of granite, nearly vertical. Ali had asked me a few times how we were going to climb it, but the truth was I had no idea. I only knew that the Bifrost bridge was supposed to extend from the top of the mountain, and I hoped we'd figure it out as we got closer.

I was certain the gods had created some sort of path; it was just a matter of finding it.

As I watched Ali climb up the trail, I could tell she was exhausted. Each step plodded in front of the other, her back slightly hunched under the weight of her pack. She wasn't accustomed to hiking miles upon miles up mountains. Now she looked like she might hobble off the trail at any moment. And I could hear her stomach growling.

Something stirred in my chest, an overpowering need to see her stop and rest. The sight of her staggering was starting to make me feel something, visceral and hot.

But whenever I suggested stopping, she tried to tell me she was fine. It seemed as Empress, she was determined to feign strength, even if she was exhausted.

"You don't have to pretend you're not tired," I said, unable to hide the irritation in my voice.

She flashed me a sour look. "Okay. I'm tired. But I just want to get there faster. The faster we stop the draugr, the better."

I looked up at the headwall looming over us. No question it was too dark to ascend it tonight. We'd have to find a place to camp.

We reached the top of the ridge, and I took in the beauty around us. Below, a small pond nestled in a hollow. A lip of rock and boulders wrapped around it, like a sort of giant nest of stone. Most importantly, I saw a large patch of alpine grass just next to the water.

I pointed to it. "I think this is the perfect place to set up camp. We can't keep climbing in the dark, Ali."

The relief on her face was apparent.

Together we stumbled down the final hundred yards of scree. I dropped my pack in the center of the grassy spot, and sat down.

Stretching out my legs, I leaned against my pack. As I stared at the last rays of the setting sun, Ali plopped down beside me, drinking water from her canteen.

When she finished, she handed it to me, and I realized my throat was parched.

Closing my eyes, I took a long slug from it. The water tasted delicious and pure. Living in Hela's realm, I'd forgotten how to enjoy anything. I'd forgotten how drinking water after a long day in the sun could be the most blissful feeling in the world.

After draining the canteen, I met Ali's gaze. She was staring at me.

I nodded at the pond. "We can refill it."

Her silver hair was stuck to her forehead, her face flushed. She slumped against her backpack, deflated. A sharp pang of guilt ran through me. I'd just drunk all her water.

Quickly I rummaged in my pack, until I found my own water bottle.

"Here," I said, handing it to her. "You can drink this. We can refill at the pond."

"Thank you." Ali immediately put it to her lips. She closed her eyes and began to drink.

I stood, refreshed by the water, and walked to the edge of the pond. A breeze ruffled its surface for a moment, dappling it with catspaws, but then it went still. Gazing into it, I could see all the way to the stony bottom.

My breath caught when I dipped my hand into the ice-cold water. As the canteen filled, I saw a flash of movement in the depths. A trout by the looks of it. How trout had made it into this tiny pond I had no idea, but I knew with certainty that I wanted Ali to eat something properly nourishing. If she was going to make it all the way to the bridge—and not slow me down—she'd need her strength.

It seemed absolutely imperative that I get this fish for her. I'd brought food with us, but it was mostly dried goods. Bread and butter, dried meat and fruit. This could be a real meal.

I watched the fish swim back and forth. I didn't have a fishing rod. Luckily, I had magic. I began to scribe the portal spell. When the fish paused for a moment, I cast the portal an inch in front of it.

Unfortunately, the portal I'd placed "in front" of the fish appeared right in the middle of its body.

There was a searing hiss of static as the exit portal appeared next to me, and half the fish shot out, projected by a jet stream of water.

Quickly, I canceled the portal. I realized that I'd forgotten to account for the difference in light refraction, the old spear fisherman's trick of aiming a foot or two in front of the fish in order to hit it in the body.

Still, it was freshly killed, and we could eat it. I picked up the fish half and walked back to the campsite.

As I approached, I saw Ali standing with her back to me, moving her arms and muttering to herself. Practicing the fire spell. I paused to watch. Her silver hair cascaded over her shoulders and down to her lower back. She'd planted her feet firmly into the grass, her leather outfit hugging her body. Even without the soul bond, I found her shockingly beautiful.

The memory of the crystal cave burst into my mind. How she'd wrapped those legs around my hips. She'd laced her fingers through my hair as I lifted her up … pressed her against the rough wall of the cave …

I shoved the thoughts away. With the mating bond severed, there was nothing between us. As she'd made clear, she felt nothing for me. She didn't want me as her mate, I was here only to help her.

What we'd had was magic, that was all. A trick of the Norns.

I dropped the meat on a nearby rock, pulled out my knife, and carefully filleted the fish. Then, I began cooking it with some fire magic, slathering it with butter from my satchel. Out of the corner of my eye I saw that Ali was watching me carefully.

"Is that a half a fish?"

"Accident when I portaled it out of the pond." She didn't look convinced. "It'll still taste good." The fish sizzled as I cooked it.

"What do you usually think about when you call fire?" asked Ali. "When you need anger?"

I suddenly realized I had no idea. I'd been scribing *kaun* for so many years, I didn't really think about it anymore. "I just get angry."

"You can get angry on command?"

"Yes." I melted more butter in a spoon, then dripped it over the fish. "We don't have any plates, we'll have to eat straight off the stone. We could go back if you like. I can make a portal and we can stay in Vanaheim tonight."

"I wasn't born an Empress. I can sleep on the ground," said Ali, again not wanting to admit any weakness. "And I don't need plates, either. I was raised on mushroom gruel." She crouched down next to me, and I handed her a fork from my bag. She was so close to me our shoulders were almost touching.

Her smell was familiar. In the cool mountain air, I felt the heat from her body radiating against me.

She swallowed a bite of fish. "This is amazing."

"I didn't want you hungry. I couldn't have you slowing me down further with your weakness." The words just came out of my mouth. I knew they were wrong somehow, yet I was broken, and they came out.

She frowned at me. "Right. Thanks."

Quickly I speared a piece of fish with my fork, and popped it in my mouth. The flavor of butter and the rich taste of the trout exploded across my palate. Until I took that bite, I hadn't realized how hungry I was.

"Hungry?" Ali asked.

"Famished."

She stared at me. "So you feel something." Her tone was

icy, but her eyes were pure fire. She was accusing me of something, and I didn't quite understand it.

All I knew was that she was right—I did feel something. And that was deeply inconvenient, because I did not want to feel a thing for her.

CHAPTER 12

ALI

The sun had set, and darkness had settled over the mountain. Galin and I sat with our rucksacks at our feet and our backs against a boulder at the edge of the grass. Faint heat radiated from the rock, built up from the sun hitting it over the course of the day, but otherwise it was freezing cold. My breath clouded every time I exhaled, and my fingers felt like icicles, even though I'd pulled my hands into the sleeves of my leather jacket. I had to grit my teeth to keep from shivering.

Galin seemed unperturbed by the drop in temperature. So he could feel things—sometimes.

Just not for me.

No matter. I didn't care one bit. I just wasn't sure I could actually sleep with my mind racing a million miles an hour. And I definitely wasn't about to admit I was cold.

Forcing myself not to think about him, I looked up into the night sky, and instead lost myself thinking about the glorious stars beaming above us. Swegde had taught me their names; the shining star he'd called Aurvandil's Toe, and the giant chariot, Karlvagn.

I pointed to Karlvagn, "Do you know the name of that constellation?"

"The Big Dipper."

I frowned. "I thought it was called Karlvagn."

"Oh, it is. The Big Dipper is the name the men of Midgard gave it." He pointed. "You see the middle star in the handle?"

"Yes."

"Is there anything unusual about it?"

I studied the star. It did seem a little odd. Blurrier than the others. I squinted. "It's two stars close together."

"That's right," said Galin. "I'm pleased you haven't lost any of your Night Elf eyesight. Men named those stars Mizar and Alcor."

"Mizar and Alcor," I repeated in a whisper.

"The little one is Alcor. It means 'forgotten' in Arabic."

There was a long pause in which we both stared at the pair of stars. After growing up in the Shadow Caverns, the night sky would never cease to amaze me.

As I studied the stars, I had the sense that Galin was looking at me. When I glanced at him, his inky eyes gleamed in the darkness. "You should sleep."

What I didn't say was that it was too cold for sleep, and that even right next to him, I felt completely alone.

I rolled over anyway, an immense wave of fatigue washing over me. My eyes closed, and I found myself drifting off—dreaming of frozen Midgard. I was walking above the Citadel, my body turning to ice. Teeth chattering, fingers going numb.

Midgard was completely abandoned now. It was just me, and the dark, winter world stretching out before me. The gods, the elves—everyone had left for another place.

The cold was going right down to my bones, ice crystallizing in my veins, and I couldn't stop the shaking—

Then, my dream shifted. The sun was rising over

Midgard, ice starting to melt. My body was thawing. For a moment, I opened my eyes, and I breathed in the scent of wood smoke—felt a powerful body move close, and steely arms wrap around me. A protective inferno of heat warmed me to my very core.

When I dreamt again, it was of spring.

* * *

"Ali," Galin whispered sharply. "Wake up."

"What—" I didn't finish as Galin's hand clamped over my mouth. My eyes snapped open.

I blinked, trying to focus. It was pitch black. It must have clouded over while I was sleeping, because the stars had disappeared. I peered blearily at my legs, noticing that Galin had placed a blanket on them at some point. Maybe that was why I'd dreamt of warmth.

That was nice of him, but it didn't explain why his hand remained latched tightly over my mouth—and my nose, too. I couldn't freaking breathe.

"Mmmhhh." I tried to speak.

Galin twisted my head to face him. He stared at me, Hela's shadow magic drifting off him, dark and mysterious. He was suffocating me.

Adrenalin filled my veins, and a terrible thought slammed into me—what if she'd asked him to assassinate me? She was his goddess. Would he do it? Bury my body under a pile of stone? Tell everyone that I'd fallen off a cliff?

If he felt nothing for me—would he do that?

I tried to open my mouth to call Skalei, but of course that didn't work. His hand was like a muzzle on my lips.

He shook his head, then a distant howl pierced the darkness, and instantly everything made a terrifying sense. He was trying to silence me, not smother me. I gripped his wrist and pulled it off, gasping for breath.

"Blooooggaaaahhh …" A second howl cut through the night. Far down the slope of the mountain, but nevertheless unmistakable. Not draugr.

Worse, much worse—the rumbling cry of a mountain troll.

"You hear that?" said Galin, finally breaking the silence.

I nodded stiffly as my heart began to slam against my ribs.

"We can't stay here," he whispered.

"Portal?"

"No time."

"BBBllooGGoogghh!" The troll's cry echoed off the rocks, the sound reverberating over my skin.

Galin stood, and I clambered up. From all the walking we'd done, my legs felt like someone had run a rolling pin all up and down them. My shoulders ached painfully where the straps of my pack had cut into them.

I hardly noticed.

Mountain trolls were out there in the darkness. Grotesque, horrifying beasts. I'd nearly been beaten to death by one once. They were literally indestructible—solid stone that even Skalei couldn't penetrate.

If they caught us, we'd be ripped limb from limb. Even Galin.

I reached to pick up my rucksack.

"No," said Galin in a sharp whisper. "Leave it."

He caught my wrist, pulling me away, towards the scree field. We ran in an all-out sprint over the craggy rocks, heading up towards the cliffs of Mount Steton.

I tried to be quiet, but the stones kept skittering out from under my feet. My heart squeezed every time I heard clicking and clacking as they bounced down the mountainside.

My lungs were heaving when we reached the ridge at the

top of the scree field. I stopped to catch my breath, and turned to look down. My heart skipped a beat. Next to our campsite was a dark form—not the boulder we'd sat against. Bigger. It had to be a troll. It moved, and I stiffened with fear.

Not one troll. Three.

Galin pulled my arm, hastening me to move again. I pumped my arms, my breath ragged in my throat. We ran along the ridgeline, up towards the talus slope. Unlike the rocky scree field, these boulders were big—nearly my height.

I took the lead then, using my night vision to find the easiest path.

Galin kept pace behind me, but every now and then I'd hear him brush against a rock in the dark, knees and shins banging into stone. But he didn't complain, just kept pushing forward.

Then, while trying to navigate a particularly awkward series of boulders, he fell flat. His head cracked loudly on a rock.

I ran to him. "Are you ok?"

"I'm fine," he said in a husky voice.

Below us, I could hear the trolls calling to one another in their howling cries, but I couldn't see them.

I grabbed Galin's wrist, somehow pulling him to his feet.

He stumbled after me as I turned again to the rocky slope. Above us, I saw a line where the jagged stones ended and the night sky began.

"I don't think it's much farther," I said.

At the top, I staggered forward, my legs rubber, lungs burning, heart hammering. I looked at my feet. The stones beneath them were smooth ... worn. I focused my eyes, and hope thrilled in my heart.

This looked like a path.

"This must lead to the summit," said Galin. A trickle of

blood ran down from his temple. He'd really taken a battering.

"I thought you knew the way?" I whispered.

"I had a general idea."

So he had no idea where we were going.

I knew he'd been keeping something from me. Was that it?

Before I could properly respond, one of the trolls howled.

"bbbBBloooogahhh!" The sound rumbled over the rocks, making the stone tremble.

I ran along the path, trying to keep my pace up, until Galin called my name. I turned to see him resting against a boulder. Blood was streaming from his forehead now.

"Are you okay?" I breathed.

"Help me push."

I realized then that he wasn't resting against the boulder —he was trying to push it over, to send it crashing down on the trolls on the slope below.

It seemed we'd run out of options, and this was the best plan we had.

I rushed over to help him, pressing my back against the boulder along with him. The chunk of rock must have weighed half a ton, but he'd gotten it partway tipped up. Planting my feet, I wedged my shoulder into the stone.

"On three," Galin gasped. "One, two." He drew in a deep breath. "Three."

I pushed up through my legs, using everything I had, like I was Atlas trying to raise the world itself. At last, the stone teetered. The path at my feet splintered.

Then suddenly the boulder toppled—too suddenly. For a moment, I lost my balance, arms windmilling, until Galin reached out and grabbed my waist.

Leaning into him, I turned to watch the boulder careening down the talus slope like a massive bowling ball, dislodging smaller boulders. In an instant, the slope became a churning deluge of falling stones, one after another.

"BBLllooggghhhAh! Blooahhggh!!!" screamed the trolls, as they were swallowed up by the landslide.

My chest unclenched, and I stared in disbelief. It had worked. The trolls were gone. The rockslide had literally scrubbed them from the face of the earth.

I suddenly realized that Galin's muscular arms were wrapped around me, holding me protectively. I pushed against him, and he immediately released me. Blood still ran down the side of his face from where he'd smashed into the rock.

"Hang on. You're trailing blood everywhere." I pulled the end of my shirtsleeve from my jacket. Standing on my tiptoes, I dabbed at Galin's forehead. He grimaced, but otherwise didn't speak.

When I pulled my arm away, my sleeve was soaked in blood. "You really need some stitches. We could portal back now."

"I heal fast." He turned away. "We need to get going. We don't know if there are any more trolls out there."

Good point. He started up the path, and I followed. This time we didn't run, but Galin kept a good pace. In front of us the massive vertical tower of stone that made up the peak of Mount Steton grew closer. At last, after a couple of switchbacks, we reached the wall.

We stood in a little dirt clearing, looking up at the cliff. A ladder had been bolted to the rock. Covered in rust and grime, it looked like it could fall apart as we used it. It shot straight up like a set of vertical train tracks until it disappeared into the darkness.

"You first." Galin gestured to the ladder.

Sucking in a deep breath, I reached for one of the rungs.

"BLOOOaaaghhGGHHH!" The sound echoed off the stone wall.

It was close. And worse—it sounded *angry*.

With a pounding heart, I leapt onto the ladder and began to climb as fast as I could.

CHAPTER 13

ALI

I raced up the ladder, hand over hand, pulling myself up as fast as I could. I was exhausted, but fortunately I could use my arms to take some of the strain off my legs. Fear and tiredness was making my legs shake.

Up here, there wasn't much to see. Directly in front of me was the cliff face—gray rock flecked with black. When I looked down over Galin, I could see the base of the cliff, and the narrow trail that had led us to this terrifying ascent.

The ladder itself was horrifying. If someone had asked me what a ladder of the gods would look like, I would have said strong and beautiful, silver metal carved with runes, steps that could support any weight. In my wildest dreams, I would never have imagined the rickety rusted crap I currently clung to.

It appeared to have been constructed by a blacksmith with a drinking problem. The rungs creaked with nearly every step. In some places the bolts and pitons that held the ladder to the rock had entirely rusted away. With every movement, it swayed, and it took nearly all my resolve to prevent myself from simply clamping my arms to its sides and freezing in place.

I glanced down to see how Galin was doing, and spotted movement at the bottom of the cliff. A shadowy mass that clarified into gray skin on a massive hulking frame, tiny red eyes that blazed with hatred. A troll had found us.

"Troll," I whispered.

"Keep going."

"Obviously."

Just as the word was out of my mouth, the troll reached for the ladder. I felt the iron rungs tremble, and I clung on for dear life as it ripped the first fifty feet of rungs clear off the cliff face.

"Blooaaarugghh!" The beast screamed in frustration.

My muscles tensed.

"Keep climbing!" Galin shouted.

But fear shot through my nerves. "Galin! Have you ever seen a troll jump?"

At exactly that moment, the troll did exactly what I'd predicted. With a grunt, it rocketed upwards until it slammed into the cliff with a tremendous crash. Dust and bits of rock sprayed everywhere, the entire wall shaking.

When the dust cleared. I saw the troll clinging to the cliff face, massive fingers digging into the rock. Its red, beady eyes stared up at us from twenty feet below.

"Blooooooarrghh!" it howled. Pure rage that rumbled through my bones.

Stone cracked as it jerked one hand from the cliff face. Then, levering itself upwards, it jabbed the hand back into the rock. Slowly it began to climb, literally carving handholds.

"Go, Ali!" shouted Galin.

I didn't need more encouragement. With a thundering heart, I rushed up the ladder, moving my hands as fast as I could. Still, I heard the troll crunching its fingers into the rock. I glanced down. The giant fucker was slowly gaining on us.

"We're going to have to fight it."

"Just keep going," shouted Galin.

I climbed another ten feet. Looked down again. Galin hung from one of the iron bars with one hand, the other frantically scribing *kaun*, the rune for fire.

"No!" I shouted. The troll was a creature of rock and stone; magma ran in its veins. The fire spell wouldn't damage it. But before I could tell Galin to stop, he sent an enormous arc of flame into the troll's face.

The fire consumed the beast, blazing like an enormous torch in the dark. Heat from the flames scalded my skin. We were in an inferno, the air scorched in all directions. Fucking hell—was *I* on fire? I couldn't breathe.

Galin flicked his wrist, and the flames went out. I found myself clinging to a burning hot ladder.

"Ow!" I shifted from one hand to another until the ladder started to cool.

Below, the troll still clung to the cliff. The top of its granite head and shoulders were blackened with soot. It didn't move. Had I been wrong about the fire?

Then it pulled its chin up from its chest. Its eyes flashed open, glowing like freshly poured ingots. It grinned, revealing a row of jagged obsidian teeth. The bastard was fine.

"Bloooaaarrrghhh!" it roared.

"Climb, Galin!" I shouted. "Fire doesn't work."

The troll lunged upwards, snatching at Galin, but it was too slow. The beast's fingers raked the rock where Galin's feet had been a moment earlier.

Galin began to climb again. Below us, the troll seemed to gather itself. I flew up the rungs of the iron ladder, fast as lightning.

"Watch out!" Galin shouted.

I glanced down, just in time to see the massive body of the troll slam into rock next to Galin, and only a few feet away from me. I yanked myself up and out of its reach, but it didn't seem interested in me.

When I looked down again, the troll was positioned just next to him. Galin was effectively cut off.

"Go, Ali!" he shouted at me. "I'll be fine."

I didn't move.

The troll grunted excitedly, then jerked one of its stony hands free of the rock. It reached for Galin.

Galin was frantically scribing, but he needed to move.

"Galin!" I screamed.

Vertigo tightened my grip as I looked straight down the cliff face. The bottom was at least five hundred feet below me. Apart from the little clearing at the base of the ladder, it was all jagged rock and stone. If I fell, I'd die.

Fighting against the vertigo, I released one of my feet. With one foot on a rung, one hand clinging to the iron, I leaned out as far as I could.

Below me a portal crackled into existence, just as the troll grabbed Galin.

"Jump, Ali!" Galin shouted. He was still clinging onto the ladder with his incredible strength, but how long would that last?

My heart was a wild beast, my body electrified with fear. If I jumped I might save myself, leaping into somewhere safe. But if I left Galin, the troll would either beat him to death or throw him from the cliff face. He'd be smashed to pieces on the rocks.

No, I'm not going to leave you behind. He was still clinging to the ladder, and there was a chance I could still save him.

Frantically, I started to scribe.

"Go, Ali!" Galin's voice sounded distant, muffled. Hanging

over the five hundred-foot drop, I focused on tracing each rune, enunciating the words of the spell. Feeling … I didn't remember what I was supposed to feel. I simply acted. I let the emotion flow from me.

At last, I finished the spell. Looked down. Nothing happened.

Then, the air began to shimmer, the familiar crackling hiss of static. I focused on expanding the portal. Two inches, three.

I could see the static now, the ring of the portal growing beneath me.

The troll grunted, beady eyes staring at the black circle.

I threw everything I had at the portal, snapping it open two feet wide. Not big enough to travel through, but that didn't matter. As it widened, it sliced into the troll's neck like the blade of a guillotine. For a second the troll's eyes widened in surprise, then the light in them started to fade. Its head pitched forward, falling into the portal.

Simultaneously, the creature's body seemed to deflate, and its grip on Galin's arm released. Molten rock spurted from the severed stump of its neck like a miniature volcano. With a final crunch of stone, it fell free. It tumbled down the cliff, spraying its burning ichor, until it slammed into the ground with a resounding thump.

Galin still gripped the ladder beneath me. "You did it!"

"Yes," I gasped, now clinging to the ladder with both hands. I felt completely drained, like I'd just run a marathon, my body vibrating with fatigue. The only thing stopping me from throwing up right now was that I'd be puking all over Galin. Was this what he experienced every time he cast a spell?

Galin's eyes shone in the darkness. "That was absolutely brilliant."

My head was spinning. "Galin. We're five hundred feet from the ground and I feel like I might faint."

"Oh, right. Of course. The first time you always give too much. It takes practice. You need to give emotion to the spell, but also regulate the amount." Galin nodded along as he spoke. "You'll get better at modulating your magic. Now you just have to practice."

"Right," I said slowly. "But I'm going to wait to think about all that until I get to the top. Because I really might hurl." Fighting the nausea, I began to climb the ladder.

One hand over another, one rung at a time—all the while pondering how I'd generated the emotion to create the spell.

Galin had said a portal spell required love.

But how exactly could that be? Our mating bond had been severed, and I didn't love anyone at all.

GALIN

I followed Ali up the ladder, unable to believe what I'd seen her do. It was one thing to try to do magic, to make the air shimmer a little, but Ali had done *real* magic. She'd created a portal using only her emotions as the source of power.

Most sorcerers practiced for months if not years before they were able to create a spell like that. And she'd cleverly used it to kill a troll. Gods, if she practiced I was certain she had the potential to be a great sorceress.

Ali moved slowly, but I didn't push her. I knew how tired she must feel. A novice sorcerer didn't know how to regulate their emotions during a spell. They simply gave everything they had.

After my first spell—ages ago—I could barely walk for a week. So even though I wanted to congratulate her, I kept quiet, and let her take her time as she climbed.

But—considering she had told me she felt nothing for me at all—I did have one burning question.

Who the fuck did she love?

Swegde? But Swegde seemed completely devoid of fun.

I pulled myself up higher, realizing that I was also completely devoid of fun. At least, I was now.

And maybe Swegde didn't say things like, "I don't want your weakness to slow me down," and, "You are a selfish wretch." Maybe he had that going for him.

As we neared the top, daylight began to filter in from the east. The rising sun warmed the air. A gentle breeze toyed with my hair. My muscles ached, and the wound in my forehead throbbed painfully, but we were almost there. I could see the top now. At most, two hundred feet to go.

Just a little farther. Once we were at the peak, I could create a portal. From there, we could go back to the temple in Vanaheim and eat some breakfast before coming back again.

And there it was again—that feeling of being hungry. Starving, even. That strange sense of caring about something. It had been a long time since I'd felt that.

One hand up, lift a foot to the next rung. Repeat with the opposite hand and foot. I kept one eye on Ali. If she slipped, I was ready to catch her.

The rising sun now warmed my back. A bird called—the sharp cry of a hawk.

Above me, Ali climbed over the last rung of the ladder and disappeared from view. Relief washed over me when I realized she'd made it, that she was safe.

"Do you see the Bifrost?" I called out as I hurried after her. Twenty more rungs, ten, five. At last, I dragged myself onto the peak of Mount Steton. I crawled forward, then slowly stood. My arms ached, even my fingers were tired from gripping the rungs of the ladder.

I rolled my shoulders, then surveyed the scene. Ali stood nearby, her silver hair alight with fire in the rising sun. In that moment, I realized how much I would hate saying goodbye to her when I left for Hel again.

Where cold ashes lay before, an ember in my chest was burning again.

Deeply inconvenient.

"How do you feel?" I asked.

"Exhausted."

I nodded. "Same."

"So what are we looking for?" asked Ali, peering about in the morning light.

"I'm not sure." The Bifrost was the road of the gods. Before Ragnarok it had been described as a shimmering path or rainbow bridge, leading from Midgard to Asgard.

I scanned the mountaintop. There was nothing like that up here. Just a lot of flat rock and debris surrounded by precipitous cliffs.

"Are you sure this is the right place?" Ali asked.

"You saw the ladder."

She raised a quizzical eyebrow. "It didn't exactly look like it was made by a god."

Good point. I frowned, closing my eyes as I racked my brain. Was the Bifrost hidden by magic? If so, I would need to know the magic word to reveal it. I wished I'd had time to do more research before coming here.

"Wait!" Ali called out. "Look at that."

I opened my eyes to see her pointing towards the edge of the cliff opposite the ladder. There was nothing there. Just empty sky. Then, the air shimmered slightly. Was there something after all?

"Do you see it?" asked Ali.

"Yes." I walked towards the cliff's edge. There definitely was something there—faint, like an oil film on water, only much more translucent. I squinted, and that helped bring it into better focus.

Nearly transparent, and hard to keep in focus, like an

afterimage from staring at the sun, but nevertheless it was clearly the shape of a bridge. It arced into the sky.

I reached out to touch it, but my fingers only passed through air.

"I can see it, but I can't feel anything," said Ali.

"Same here. Maybe because it was destroyed in Ragnarok."

"Can you fix it?"

I tried to touch it again, the remnants of magic raising the hair on my arms.

"Yes, I believe I could. It's actually quite a lot like the wall spell I created."

Gilded in the sunlight, she nodded. "The one to trap the Night Elves."

"Unfortunately there's a problem. It took me months to design that spell. To fix this"—I gestured to the mirage—"would take years."

She dropped her head into her hands. "So we need a new plan."

CHAPTER 15

ALI

I stared at Galin, my mind whirling. Was that what he was keeping from me—that he didn't really know the route across the Bifrost bridge? That he'd possibly lead me up here, past trolls and explosions, for nothing?

No. I thought there was more. "What else are you not telling me?"

His eyes glinted. "There was a time when you might have known instinctively, and when you could have demanded that I tell you things. With our mating bond severed, that time is over."

Great.

"I guess we need to go back, then. We need a new plan." My tone sounded icy. "We don't have years to spend here. You know, you could have mentioned this in the planning stages, that maybe there was no bridge left? We just wasted time." I wondered if I had enough anger in me now to summon fire magic. "Every day that we lose, the draugr will get closer."

He folded his arms, the wintry wind whipping at his dark hair. "I could have learned this faster alone. You were the one who insisted on coming."

I sighed, reminding myself of how quickly he'd moved on. Yes—he was defying Hela by trying to defeat the draugr. But he was also her consort. She was his queen, his lover. Thinking of them together, I shuddered.

And worse—I knew that he was keeping more secrets from me.

As my mood grew darker, Galin drew another portal. I sighed as it crackled into existence. I wasn't looking forward to telling the council we were coming back empty-handed. Still, I was alive. We'd just have to figure out something else, because letting the draugr overrun us was not an option.

Galin gestured at the portal. With a final glance at the barren peak of Mount Steton, I stepped through the magic opening. And as I did, my stomach flipped.

Where were we?

Smoke filled the air, and it smelled absolutely terrible. It took me a moment to recognize the sandstone walls, the familiar bird cages. We'd come to my quarters. But what had once been my favorite sofa now smoldered, and burn marks scorched the walls. Strangest of all, a small boulder lay in the middle of the room.

My heart started to hammer, breath shallowing. What the fuck?

Something had gone terribly wrong in my absence.

I looked around, quickly checking for danger. Was this a stone from a catapult? Were we under attack? Were there draugr in the temple? Could draugr build catapults?

"Skalei." I felt the hilt of my blade arrive in my palm.

I glanced at the portal in time to see Galin arrive. "Galin," I whispered. "I think we may have been attacked by draugr."

He turned, surveying the damage. In a flash, his eyes moved from the burned sofa, to the walls, to the rock in the middle of the rug.

"Ali," said Galin, failing to hide a tone of laughter, "there's nothing to worry about."

"What do you mean? My room has been burned and pillaged."

He nodded at the rock. "Where did you send that troll's head?"

I grimaced, only now noticing that I was looking at stretched gray skin. "No …"

"You sent it here." He gestured to some gray dust on the sofa. "This was the troll's blood that spurted into the portal. It's blazing hot. You're lucky you didn't burn down the entire temple."

As I exhaled slowly, my eye fell on the shelf where I'd been storing my vergr crystal. The entire wall had been ripped open, and shattered crystal twinkled on the ground. Piles of ashes and rubble covered this part of the room. I'd sent the freaking portal through the shelf with the vergr stones. If Barthol tried to get back now, he'd be split into a million pieces.

My throat tightened. "Oh, fuck."

I picked up one end of the burned shelf. As I did, a stone slid towards the floor from under the ashes. Galin's hand shot out to catch it.

When I examined it more closely, I could tell by the size it was Barthol's.

I bit my lip. "I guess I need to practice the precision of that spell."

Brushing the ash off myself, I turned and crossed to the door. The guard standing before the door turned to look at me, his eyes wide.

"Empress, are you all right?" Worry etched his features as he tried to determine how much trouble he was in. "Empress, I'm so sorry. I'm not allowed to enter your quarters without permission—"

"Don't worry about it. It's just a decapitated troll's head that I sent through a portal. Normal stuff. Might need a bit of a cleanup. A cleaning and repair crew has my permission to enter."

He stared at me as I turned to cross down the hallway, already thinking about what I'd tell the council. I might leave out the specifics of the troll's head.

* * *

WHEN WE REACHED the council chambers, I paused at the door, my stomach tight. I was supposed to be returning victorious, with information on how to stop the draugr horde. Instead we'd barely escaped with our lives, and been unable to cross the Bifrost.

I was reaching to push open the doors when Galin said, "Ali, before you go in, let me give you some advice. There's telling the whole truth, and then there's telling the relevant truth."

"What?"

Without further explanation, he went inside. The full contingent of the council sat at the table, surrounded by fresh bread and fruit. Apparently, we'd come into the room while they were in the process of eating breakfast.

For a long moment no one spoke, their eyes moving between Galin and me with increasing degrees of concern. Then Sigre dropped a spoon, and that broke the spell.

Swegde jumped up. "What happened? Did you learn how to defeat the draugr?"

"We hiked all day, Galin caught a fish but he accidentally cut it in half. But the thing is, that saved his life later because if he hadn't shown me what a portal spell could do, he would have been killed by the troll—"

"A troll?" Swegde cut in.

Galin held up his hands. "We ran into some difficulties, but no one was hurt."

"You have blood all over your face," said Sigre.

"I ran into a rock," said Galin. Then, defensively, "It was dark."

"You ran into a rock …" Swegde repeated slowly, like he was trying to decipher a foreign language.

"In any case," I said, using my *in-charge-Empress* voice, "We didn't make it to Asgard."

"I gathered as much," said Swegde.

"What about the Bifrost bridge?" asked Bo.

I sighed. "It's almost completely destroyed. Ragnarok wrecked it. Galin says it would take years to repair it. We need a plan B."

Swegde shook his head. "There isn't another way to get to Asgard. Only the Bifrost, or a portal if someone had been there." He frowned. "Gods weren't really very big on visitors."

I rubbed a knot in my forehead. "Any estimates on how long we have before the draugr overrun our gates?"

"Maybe two weeks," Swegde said quietly.

Balls. I racked my brain. "What about animals?"

The entire council stared at me like I'd lost my mind.

I cleared my throat. "Well, I remember hearing the great squirrel Ratatoskr brought messages to an eagle that lives at the top of Yggdrasill. And the eagle once spoke to the gods, when they were alive. That means the eagle can fly to Asgard."

Silence filled the room, and frustration simmered. They thought I was crazy. "Ratatoskr is still climbing up and down Yggdrasill. There is every reason to think the eagle is still there, too."

Galin scrubbed a hand over his jaw, studying me. "It's not a bad idea."

"Empress." Sigre flicked her blonde hair over her shoulder. "This is even crazier than trying to cross the Bifrost."

Galin glared at her. "All of this is insane, including the draugr invasion. And yet it's happening anyway."

I crossed my arms. "So if we went to the Well of Wyrd, we could climb back out on Ratatoskr. This time, we let him take us all the way to the top of the tree. If the eagle isn't there, we just portal back again."

Swegde had gone pale, and he rose from his chair. "What you're proposing is returning to the bottom of the Well of Wyrd, finding and then riding a vicious giant squirrel to the top of Yggdrasill, where you're hoping to convince a giant eagle to fly you to Asgard?"

"Yes," Galin and I answered at the same time.

CHAPTER 16

ALI

An hour later, I stepped through a new portal and into the cavern at the roots of Yggdrasill. It was just as I remembered, dark and wet, with the smell of rotting wood permeating the air.

Galin's portal had placed me on top of one of the giant roots, and beneath my feet I could feel the humming tree-magic. A massive pile of bones in the center of the clearing rose high above us.

As I surveyed the now familiar space, Galin appeared next to me. With a quick flick of his fingers he cast *sowilo*, and a glowing rune appeared above us to cast more light.

The pile of bones was huge. Femurs, skulls, ribs … how many elves had died to build it this high? I wasn't sure I wanted to think about that. My stomach clenched at the horror of falling to death in this lonely place.

"The dead here," I whispered. "It was mostly executions, right? By King Gorm?"

"Yes," said Galin softly. He gazed at the bones, his expression unreadable. Black vapor from his chest tattoos swirled round him ominously. At last he spoke again. "It's a terrible legacy for my family."

I sighed. "That, and the Night Elves Gorm hunted."

If it weren't for Galin, the High Elves would have destroyed my people completely. There would be no Night Elves for me to protect. I glanced at him, a strange thought striking me like a diamond bullet. If it weren't for Galin, I wouldn't even exist.

I studied him—dark hair, broad shoulders. He met my gaze, and I felt like his eyes were piercing enough to penetrate my soul.

For just a moment, I felt as if we were connected again—my soul to his. No one else could compare to him, but he was scarred. Imprisoned for a thousand years, his mother and father murdered, raised by cruel and savage High Elves. He'd been forced to protect himself among the enemy. No wonder he'd taken to magic. Not just for self-preservation; it must have been an escape, a way to add order and purpose to his life.

There were walls around him—and not just magical ones. He was adrift.

I pulled my gaze away from him. "As Empress of the Vanir and leader of the elves, let me formally thank you for your sacrifice when you put up the walls to protect the Night Elves from King Gorm."

When I met his gaze again, he was staring at me, eyes gleaming like burnished obsidian.

Then, a smile ghosted over his lips. "Would the Empress of the Vanir like to formally join me on a giant squirrel?"

"Of course."

I walked at his side, past the elven remains. There must have been ten thousand bodies in the massive unorganized ossuary.

I could see where Ratatoskr had bashed the pile when it first attacked—back when we'd visited Yggdrasill. The creature had broken and scattered the bones like a dropped box of matchsticks. Glowing sap still dripped from the wound where its saw-like teeth had carved a six-foot hole into one of the roots.

As we walked around the bone pile, I looked out for signs of the squirrel, but the place seemed silent as a grave.

When Galin stopped, I followed his gaze to a black patch next to a broken femur. He cocked his head, staring at dried blood spread over the bones.

"What is it?" I asked.

"This was where I fell."

I sucked in a breath. "This is *your* blood?"

Galin nodded.

An ache welled in my chest, and I wished I could go back in time to stop it from happening. "Is this where Hela found you?"

"The shade Ganglati found me. Still alive."

"You must have been …" I trailed off. When I saw Galin fall into the Well of Wyrd that final time, I'd assumed that he died instantly, that the impact killed him. It was only after I came back to check that I started to have hope again.

But while he'd been down here, gravely injured, he must have thought he would die alone. And then Ganglati came, and brought him to Hel. No wonder he agreed to serve as Hela's king, her consort. She was his salvation.

"I wish I'd found you sooner. I don't like thinking of you lying broken down here."

Galin shrugged. "The important thing was that you were safe."

I'd already severed the soul bond by the time Galin fell into the Well of Wyrd. He shouldn't have cared whether I lived or died.

Earlier, he'd said he didn't feel a thing. Had he been lying?

He turned from me and shouted into the darkness. "Ratatoskr!" His voice echoed off the walls, but not another sound. "Let me try again." He drew in a deep breath. "Raataa-tooooskrrrr!"

I winced at the sound, much louder this time. Still the squirrel didn't come barreling out of the darkness.

"Let me try."

Galin nodded. I shouted *Ratatoskr* a few times, but nothing moved in the shadows beyond Galin's magical light.

"Wait." I touched his arm. "What if we do the squirrel call? Remember how it screamed when it attacked us? Maybe we need to speak its language."

"I had no voice for a thousand years. I'll need you to attempt that."

I cleared my throat, straightening. Then I cupped my hands around my mouth, and screamed. "Kuk kuk tzztzt tzt zzzzzttt!"

The sound reverberated in the cavern until only silence remained. Still, there was no sign of the squirrel.

"Maybe it needs more Kuks?" Galin offered.

I tried again, over and over, my voice echoing, throat getting dry. When it was clear nothing was happening, I plopped down on the tree root. "I don't think it's coming."

Galin turned to me, eyes alert. "Do you know what? We can use a moth."

And without another word, he was already scribing a portal.

CHAPTER 17

ALI

Ten minutes later, my legs were wrapped around the body of a giant moth—and my arms wrapped around Galin's chiseled abs. My thighs were pressed against his as we flew through the air.

We swept over the bone pile, then Galin pulled back on the moth's antenna, and we began to climb, nearly vertical. I tightened my grip around his stomach. My hair whipped behind me. And despite the obvious danger of what we were doing, I felt secure this close to Galin.

Quickly Yggdrasill's roots disappeared into the shadows of the cave. For a long time we simply climbed in tar-black air.

Even with my night vision, the cavern was so dark, so large, I could hardly see a thing. It was like the bottom of the sea, no sensory input beyond the rhythmic beating of the moth's wings. I pressed my head against Galin's back. With my ear on his skin, I could feel his heart beating, strangely comforting. When I first met him, his heart hadn't beat at all. Now, I felt in tune with the rhythm of his blood.

Every now and then, he would adjust his grip on the

antenna, and I could feel the thickly corded muscles shift in his core. His smoky scent wrapped around me.

When I looked up over his shoulder, I saw the first tree branch, looming out of the darkness—large as a bus, and directly above our heads.

"Galin! Watch out!"

Galin jerked the moth's antenna hard to the right, and we just barely avoided slamming into the branch. Once we'd cleared it, Galin called over his shoulder, "Can you use your Night Elf vision to look out for more of those things?"

"On it."

We climbed higher, and I shifted even closer to him, nestling my chin over his shoulder. I focused on looking out for Yggdrasill's branches. Eventually, light began to filter in from above, and it became easier to see. Galin directed the moth higher and higher, easily avoiding the branches on his own.

A breeze began to rush over us, and I could sense the moth struggling, its flight more erratic. As we flew higher, the branches thinned, and Galin directed the moth to land on one of them. It slowly glided down to rest on the bark.

Only then did I realize I was out of breath from the effort of holding onto the moth with my body. Slowly, I unclenched my arms from Galin. He slid off first, and I followed, touching down on the branch.

"We should ascend on our own now." He looked up at the branches, spaced far apart. Climbing would not be easy. "I can shadow jump from one to another. And when I get up, I'll reach for you. It will be the fastest way."

Before I could utter another word, he flickered out of existence in a haze of smoke. He reappeared again, face down on a branch, arm extended to me. On my tiptoes, I reached up and gripped his forearm. For a moment, I was filled with the dizzying fear that I could fall to my death with one slip—plummeting hundreds of feet to that bloodied pile of bones. But then Galin pulled me up with his tremendous strength, until I could grab hold of the branch myself and swing my leg over.

We moved like that, from one branch to another, until we'd built a sort of rhythm together—shifting between limbs. But as we climbed, gusts of wind began to rush over us, making it harder to stay balanced. Then, I'd cling to the branches, or to Galin.

I started to see glimpses of the sky between Yggdrasill's massive leaves—a strange but beautiful inky black night, punctuated with stars so vivid they nearly hurt my eyes.

As I slid my leg over onto one of the enormous branches, I stopped to catch my breath, looking up at the glittering sky. When I glanced at Galin again, he was silvered in the starlight, the light and shadow sculpting his cheekbones, glinting in his dark eyes.

"Beautiful, isn't it? I said. A thousand years in a prison cell, and I didn't see starlight the entire time. I couldn't remember what I was missing, either. But I was missing it all the same."

"But I've never seen stars like these before."

"Me neither." He met my gaze and quirked a smile. "But I was missing them all the same, even if I didn't know it yet." His deep, velvety voice skimmed over my skin, making goosebumps rise.

I wasn't sure why his words made my heart race faster, but they did. With a great deal of effort, I pulled my gaze away from him again.

As we stared up at the sky, a shadow blotted out some of the stars. At first I thought it was a cloud, but it moved too quickly. A black silhouette against the sky.

"Do you see that?" I pointed. "What is it?"

"Maybe the eagle." Galin reached up to a branch above his head. "If we keep climbing, maybe we'll find out."

One branch after another, we kept moving up the tree—Galin shadow jumping, leaning down to pull me up—until the dark shape loomed above us. The eagle? No—not the right shape, and it was completely still.

As Galin hoisted me up, I slid in close to him on the branch. "Is that a nest?" I whispered.

"I think so."

It was two more branches before we reached the branch below it, and it spread out far and wide above us. The size of a city block, close enough that Galin could reach up and touch it. It seemed to be blocking our way.

"Can you get past it? With your jumping through space thing?"

He shook his head. "I need to see where I'm jumping to. And I can't portal any higher without having been there before. We will need to find another way."

A normal bird's nest is made of sticks and twigs. This one seemed to be made of massive pieces of wood, many nearly as thick around as my arm. They were jumbled together in a disorganized heap. Still, when Galin reached up to tug one, the wood didn't budge.

"Seems solid." Galin looked out towards the edge of the nest. "We'll have to climb around the outside."

I followed his gaze. It seemed possible—but dangerous as Hel. We'd have to trust that the wood of the nest was strong enough to support our weight. And at the same time? We'd have to hang thousands of feet above the ground. A fall would mean instant death—shattered on the old elf bone pile.

"Maybe there's another way." I peered into the bottom of the nest, eyeing the gaps. Were they big enough to climb through? I thought I saw a crevice twisting up into the starry sky.

"I think we might be able to squeeze through."

"If the wood shifts—"

"We get crushed by logs. But you said it seems solid, right?"

I narrowed my eyes. "No, but I can go first. I'm smaller, and used to being in little cave-like areas."

He stared at me for a long time, seemingly considering this. Rays of starlight beamed through the cracks in the nest. "This could be dangerous. I don't want anything happening to you."

I felt my cheeks warm. "You need to trust me."

At last, he nodded. "I'll lift you up."

He reached down for my waist, his powerful hands wrapping around me. For just a moment, I let my gaze roam over his shoulder muscles, his chest. Then, he lifted me up, and I reached for the nest, gripping onto one of the logs. Galin continued lifting me. I tried not to think of the feel of his hands on my thighs, because I needed to focus. After all the climbing, my arm muscles burned. But at last, I had a secure grip on the wood.

It was dark, but my Night Elf vision had no trouble illuminating the interior. The crack quickly narrowed, but by dropping to my stomach I was able to squeeze through. Above me I could see light, and the passage widened—large enough for Galin. It would work.

"It's a bit tight," I called down, "but you should be able to do it."

I pulled myself in farther. Twisting between the massive pieces of wood, I made my way higher until I was able to poke my head through into the bottom of the nest, my shoulders above the surface.

Above me the night sky spread out in a glorious sea of

stars, but I only gave them a quick glance. Instead I focused on the nest. It was a large platform, about half the size of a football field, made up of a sort of thatch of tree trunks. I guessed I could walk across it, but it would be tricky. One slip and I could break an ankle.

The surface was marred by strange lumps. Large mushrooms maybe? And in one corner a great tuft of feathers.

It smelled of death—incongruent with the beautiful scene of stars above. It took me a few seconds to realize that the bumps I'd thought were large mushrooms were actually large animal bones, picked clean. Cow bones, I thought. Disturbing.

I looked down again, relieved to see Galin pulling himself up next to me. His head breached the surface, and he surveyed the grim scene before us.

We were squished together now, my body pressed against his.

"A graveyard for cows," he murmured.

"Do you think they're from Vanaheim?" Swegde would be upset to learn that an eagle was eating our cattle. "And look over there." I pointed to the large clump of feathers.

Galin grabbed me and pushed my head down, just as the nest shifted. There was a rush of wind, and the whole structure shook as if in a storm.

As the nest teetered, I gripped onto Galin. A deafening shriek nearly shattered my eardrums.

"SKREEEEEeee!"

And there's our eagle. The creature blotted out the stars above us as it settled into the nest. It dropped what I thought was a dead cow from its talons. Then, a giant black eye peered into the crevice where Galin and I were hiding. Unfortunately, it did not seem happy to see us.

"Scree! Screeeee!" it screamed.

"It's huge," I whispered.

"So was Ratatoskr," said Galin. "We will be okay."

The giant eagle hopped around, peering at us from between the branches as it continued to scream and squawk.

"Your fingernails are digging into me," said Galin.

"Oh, right." I unclenched them from his skin, but I was still holding tight to his enormous shoulders. My legs were wrapped around his abs, toes lodged into the wood to keep me steady.

Above us, the giant eagle picked up the cattle carcass. The bird's head was the size of a small car, its beak larger than Galin. I winced, expecting to see a gush of gore as it consumed the dead cow, but instead it jerked its head and flung the carcass from the nest.

Tilting its head back, it screamed angrily into the starry sky.

"What's going on?" I asked Galin. "Why didn't it eat the dead cow?"

Galin frowned. "I'm not sure."

"So what do we do now? Do we have a way to communicate with it?"

Galin smiled. "Yes. Give me a second." He stared into my eyes. "But you'll need to release your arms from my shoulders, and hold the wood. Tight."

I shifted off him, letting my legs fall. I got a solid foothold. When I turned back to look at him, I heard the electric pop of a portal, and he was gone.

I tried not to think about what would happen if he didn't return. But I didn't have to worry long either way, because he was back within moments.

"What's going on?" I asked. Almost without thinking, I wrapped my arms around his shoulders again. Somehow, I felt safest that way.

With a faint smile, he held up a strange purplish vial.

"What is it?" I asked, feeling thoroughly confused.

"Dragon blood. You will want to let go of me again. Get a good foothold, and try to cover your ears."

I released him again, finding a steady spot. "What are you talking about?"

Before I could ask any more questions, he tilted back his head and slugged the contents of the vial down. Based on the grimace on his face, I guessed it tasted terrible.

But that was nothing compared to what happened when he opened his mouth and spoke.

Instead of words he screamed, "SKREEE!"

CHAPTER 18

GALIN

Speaking in the tongue of birds was never a pleasant experience. Firstly, dragon blood tasted absolutely terrible. Hot and bitter, like drinking a shot of boiling-hot pine sap. I had to fight my gag reflex, just to keep it down. Secondly, eagles talked like someone was drawing a dagger across their throat.

It literally hurt to speak.

But if I wanted to get Ali safely up to Asgard, my vocal chords were going to have to suffer.

"We aren't here to hurt you," I screeched in the language of eagles. "We merely wish to ask a small favor."

At last the eagle replied, "What want?"

"Passage to Asgard."

The eagle laughed, a terrifying sound, high pitched and demented. "Not a carriage."

"You are our only hope."

The eagle lowered its face to the crevice, and fixed me with a massive yellow eye. "Asgard ruined. No gods. Only sons of Fenrir."

"It is imperative that we go as soon as possible."

"Cannot help." The eagle flapped its wings, and the nest shook as though in a hurricane. "Must hunt. Hungry."

I needed to stall. If the eagle left, I had no idea how long it would be before it returned. "Why did you throw that carcass away?"

"Rotten. I am not a vulture." The eagle screeched loudly—the equivalent of profanity in bird language.

"Then why did you bring it here?"

"The army of the dead eat the great herds. Not much left."

The eagle flapped its wings again. The nest shook to a terrifying degree, and I slid my arm around Ali's waist, pulling her tight to me. More than ever, I felt an over-whelming need to get her to safety. Not just now, but for as long as I could. I *had* to stop the draugr.

"We wish to help stop the plague of the dead," I shouted in Eaglish.

The eagle cocked its head, but its gaze continued to follow me with an unnerving intensity. If I didn't convince it to help us in the next breath, it was definitely going to try to eat me.

"What's going on?" Ali whispered.

"The eagle is starving. The draugr have been killing its cattle, and I believe it wants to eat us."

"Tell it that I'll let it feed from my herds as much as it likes, if it helps us. And that we will stop the draugr from ruining the cattle."

The eagle crouched, preparing to strike.

"Wait!" I shouted. "This is the Empress of the Vanir, she says you may feast on her cattle if you help us. We will stop the armies of the dead, and keep you fed."

The eagle's beak lowered into the crevice.

I sensed that the cattle wouldn't be enough. "And I wish to raise the gods, to bring Ragnarok to an end."

"What?" asked Ali.

The eagle's head jerked back. "You lie?"

"I am a sorcerer. I want the gods to return just as much as you do."

"I eat cattle and my friends return? The gods?"

"Yes."

The eagle pressed its eye against the crevice.

"Nod your head," I whispered sharply to Ali.

She nodded like her life depended on it.

"Agreed," said the eagle with a croaking squawk.

It pulled its head away from the crevice at last.

My chest unclenched with relief. I pulled myself out of the passage, and turned to grab Ali's arm. Just as I got her out, I felt a claw closing around me, and I stared as another gripped Ali.

With a great beat of its wings, the eagle lifted us into the air.

I *had* been hoping to ride on its back, but undignified transportation would have to do.

* * *

THE GREAT EAGLE beat its wings in a deafening cacophony of rushing air as we lifted off from the nest. It held each of us tightly in a clawed foot. Pounding the air, it rose above Yggdrasill. For the first time, I could see the tree in its epic majesty, bathed in starlight—a massive ash that dwarfed any living thing I'd ever seen. The dragon Niddhogg would have been but a worm in its roots.

Gaining altitude, the eagle spread its wings and began to glide silently through the air. As we rose higher and higher, it adjusted its grip. Now, it gently curled the toes of each foot into a sort of cage that we could sit in. It was actually quite comfortable—as long as you didn't stick yourself on the end of one of its talons.

Yggdrasill disappeared below us as we flew into the space between worlds. An inky darkness surrounded us, and stars flickered above and below, as if we swam in an ocean of bioluminescent sea creatures.

I glanced at Ali. She sat like me, cozy in the curl of the eagle's other claw. Her silver hair spilled out behind her in the astral wind, and her eyes shone in the starlight. She was shockingly beautiful, and I'd hardly been able to think straight when her arms and legs were wrapped around me, body pressed against me. In Hel, I thought my soul had died again—that I'd stopped desiring anything. But now? My mind whirled with all the things I'd like to do to her if she were still my mate.

If she were. I had to forget that though, because she was no longer mine.

"Galin," she called out through the wind. "Have you ever seen anything like this?"

I was about to say no, when I realized that this place was actually familiar. I *had* seen something like this. "If the stars were souls," I called out, "this would be just like traveling to the astral plane."

Ali peered at me through the eagle's talons. "Maybe they are."

I looked up to the stars. Without any ground below us or clouds above, there was no horizon, no way to calibrate my depth perception. The stars could be a billion light years away, or only just beyond the reach of my fingertips. Was it possible that they weren't stars at all? Could the stars really be souls? Were we actually flying through the astral plane itself?

I supposed I could check by ascending, but I realized I didn't care. The view was extraordinary, and I didn't want to miss a minute of it.

"You could be right," I said at last.

"How did you become a sorcerer?" she called. "Who taught you?"

I stared into the stars, my mind swelling with long-forgotten memories. Learning magic had been the most extraordinary experience of my life. Terribly hard, but also incredibly rewarding. More than that, it had given me purpose, a sense of identity. A sorcerer was what I *was*; I would never not be one.

But it was also inextricably tied up in loss, in death. I didn't want to think about that now, not when I flew in the ether that surrounded the nine worlds. And I didn't want to think about my other loss—my soul mate. If she were still mine—at the first chance I got—I'd be pinning her up against a wall, claiming her mouth. I'd make her gasp. Because mating bond or not, spending time around her had lit a fire in my chest, and I wasn't sure it would ever go out.

But she was gone now, too. So I would burn for her, and I would never tell a soul what I felt.

She had made her choice, and I would honor that.

I tried to ignore the sharp pain in my chest as I said, "My mother taught me magic."

"Your mother?" said Ali, sounding surprised.

"She showed me how to use my emotions for magic."

One of Ali's eyebrows flicked up. "So what do you think of when you cast the fire spell?"

"Honestly, so many terrible things have happened to me, that anger is an emotion that I can channel at will."

Ali frowned, unsatisfied with my answer. "What about the portal spell? You have to feel love to cast that one, right?"

I took a sharp breath. "I use Hela's magic. Before that, I scribed my first portal spell when I was seventeen, a week after my mother died. Only when she died did I understand love."

I looked at her, ten feet from me, clasped in the eagle's

foot. Her eyes shone now in the starlight. My chest ached, like I'd been carved open, and I wanted to change the subject. "The light spell—*swilio*—the one I cast at the roots of Yggdrasill, you just have to feel happy. I think about the time King Gorm's trousers split during an important meeting, and he accidentally mooned the room. And there's a spell for darkness that's powered by sadness."

"If anger causes fire, what causes ice?" asked Ali.

"There is no cold spell," I called out. "We might have lost some knowledge. Long ago, there were entire magical families that worked together. Brothers and sisters, fathers and mothers. They could do exceptionally powerful magic. Fire spells so hot they could melt diamonds, light spells so bright they outshone the stars, but they were extremely secretive. With their deaths, their spells and methods were lost. No one knows how they did it. There are tons of stories like that. Witches and sorcerers with great powers and spells that were forgotten."

"And I thought sorcerers wrote everything down in grimoires and spell books ..." She trailed off, looking below us.

I followed her gaze down. Sure enough, there was something there, a darkening in the stars.

The eagle's wings moved, and we began to descend.

I called up to it in the language of eagles, "What is it?"

My heart thrilled at the great raptor's answer. "Asgard."

CHAPTER 19

ALI

I leaned forward, looking between the eagle's claws. Even though the bird could drop me at any time, I felt safe.

A shape loomed in the darkness. When I'd first spotted it, it was nothing more than a black smudge. Only now as we grew closer did it become more distinct, like an enormous pile of gray cotton candy miles below us.

Clouds.

The eagle swooped lower. My hair flew back, and my ears filled with the rushing sound of wind as we passed into the clouds. From high up they'd looked soft and fluffy, but now that we were within them I quickly discovered they were wet and cold. I shivered involuntarily.

I glanced over at Galin, but he was staring intently straight ahead, unaffected by the cold.

As we swept lower, the eagle screamed. We burst free of the clouds, just above a churning gray sea. Pale vapor swirled above the roiling waves.

When I envisioned Asgard, I'd always imagined a beautiful city, marble buildings and golden roofs. Ice-cold water and iron-gray crashing waves had never been part of the picture. Freezing sea spray spattered us, even from here. I licked my lips, tasting salt. The air smelled of brine.

The eagle's wings beat loudly as it raced over the ocean, only a hundred feet above the waves. In the distance grew a shadowy darkness. Land, I realized, as almost simultaneously we soared over it. The eagle banked sharply, then slowed.

Asgard.

Below us, a massive city spread out—or what was left of it. It was immediately clear that Ragnarok and the years that followed had taken their toll. What once must have been the gold and gleaming city of my dreams was now a jumble of broken stones and twisted metal. My throat tightened as I took in the damage.

The only thing intact was the castle looming at one end.

The eagle brought us down just outside the city walls, in a barren landscape of empty fields and rocks. Hovering for a moment, wings beating mightily, it gently set us down on the ground. As I stumbled forward, the eagle's wings churned the air. With a final avian scream, it disappeared into the clouds.

Galin crossed to me, seawater sliding down his muscles in rivulets. Even now, even with the mating bond severed, tearing my gaze off his perfect form was a trial worthy of the gods. I felt the strongest urge to cozy up to him for warmth, but I resisted.

Stiff from the ride in the eagle's claws, I rolled my shoulders to loosen my muscles. Then, I studied our surroundings. We were in a large field before Asgard's city walls. Not nearly as big as the wall that surrounded Hel, but definitely too big to climb—especially after what we'd already been through.

I hugged myself, starting to walk. "There must be a gate somewhere."

As Galin and I walked, a statue came into view. The enormous sculpture was in ruins, with no head or arms. Only the massive marble hammer resting on the ground made it clear who it was at once. A sense of reverence whispered over my skin, raising the hair on my nape. I was shivering from more than just the cold.

"Thor," I murmured. This had once been his home—the strongest of all the gods.

Galin nodded. Then he pointed farther down the wall, where a second statue stood. Weathered and missing an arm, he wore an eye patch.

"Odin," Galin said in a low, quiet voice. God of wisdom.

A shiver of excitement rippled through me at being here on this sacred ground, even if the gods were dead.

"Where do you think we find the Well of Knowledge?" I whispered. I had no idea why I was whispering. We were the only living people here, and yet I felt like I was trespassing.

"I don't know yet," said Galin. He winced, rubbing his throat. The eagle cries had apparently wrecked his vocal cords. "But I think we'll find what we need in Bilskirnir." He pointed over the city walls, where the golden roof of the castle rose into the night sky.

From the air it had been obvious that the castle was large, but the true vastness of its size only became more apparent from the ground. The marble tower was massive. At least as big around as Boston's Citadel, but much taller. Wisps of clouds drifted past it, nearly obscuring the roof.

We walked along the marble wall, passing more statues. A goddess holding out a box in one hand: Frigg, the wife of Odin. Her sister Freya, seductive clothing wrapped around her body. A lithe god holding a wand who I guessed was Loki, son of the gods' worst enemies, the Jötunn giants. Loki —father of my new rival.

It took me a while to realize that mounds swelled the ground before each statue. "Are these graves, Galin?"

He glanced at me, nodding solemnly.

At last, we reached a gate in the wall—iron doors, wide

open. I held my breath as we crossed between them into the ancient, abandoned streets of Asgard.

Crumbling ruins lay before us—buildings missing walls, rubble littering the streets. But it was impossible not to see what it once had been. We walked down wide avenues paved with fine marble.

Dim light filtered in through the gray clouds. A clammy fog drifted between the broken buildings, and there was no sign of life here—no birds, no living trees. The broken roofs and rubble were a constant reminder that something that had once been great now lay in ruins.

As we moved deeper into the city, the buildings grew larger, and a feeling of unease began to crawl over me. I had a creeping sense that we weren't wanted here. It was as if the ghosts of the dead gods were watching us, telling us to leave.

"Ali," said Galin in a raspy whisper. "If something goes wrong and I make a portal, I want you to go through it straight away, okay? Don't even wait for me." His eyes shone fiercely.

"Okay." I didn't really mean it. I might be an Empress now, but I wasn't going to leave Galin behind. If shit did hit the fan, I could at least call Skalei and try to kill someone. I'd make my own determination as to when I'd be diving through a portal to safety.

Above us the walls of Bilskirnir loomed ever closer. Massive and imposing, it rose from the ground like a giant obelisk. In its heyday, shining and new, I imagined it must have rivaled the gods themselves. Now the stone was stained with age, and in places there were great scars in its marble walls, as if some giant beast had once sharpened its claws on it.

As we made our way toward the castle, the clouds thickened and the sky grew darker. Rain began to fall, a light drizzle that quickly became a drenching torrent.

"Hurry." Galin picked up the pace.

A rumble of thunder boomed over the horizon. And then, even farther off, another noise. Not thunder, but a howl.

"Fenrir's children," Galin said quietly.

His words sent a shudder of dread through my body. For the briefest instant, his face was illuminated by a flash of lightening. Water dripped from his wet hair as he looked behind me. Real concern glinted in his eyes—and at that moment, I knew Fenrir's children were terrifying.

We raced along the marble streets, their howls growing closer. Galin in the lead, his broad shoulders carving a path through the rain, and I running just behind him.

I tried to remember what I knew of Fenrir. If the stories were true, then he'd been one of Hela's brothers. Not a man, but a giant wolf who'd killed Odin, who'd ravaged the world during Ragnarok. Which meant that Fenrir's children were likely wolves.

Another howl cut through the storm.

A crackling bolt of lightning struck a rooftop a few streets away, illuminating everything in a strobing flash of light. Raindrops hung suspended in the air; the water sloshing from the rooftops appeared frozen, like icicles. In the distance, a furry creature ducked behind a building. Fear clutched at my heart. The wolf was several stories tall.

Galin held a finger to his lips, then beckoned me to follow him.

He cut away from the main boulevard, and we sprinted along dimly lit side streets, sticking to the shadows. The rain fell hard and cold. If we hadn't been running, I would have been shivering uncontrollably.

Galin yanked me into an ancient doorway, clamping a hand to my mouth. An instant later, another lightning strike revealed the silhouette of a massive wolf's head the next street over. I turned, and we started running again.

One leg in front of the other, lungs heaving, freezing water soaking my skin, I kept pace with Galin. In the distance, Bilskirnir grew larger, even as around us a cacophony of terrible howls rose.

"They're hunting," Galin rasped, his voice ragged.

I didn't answer, just fought to keep running.

Behind us the voices of the wolves formed a deafening chorus. I counted five or six of them at least.

The storm was directly over us now. Lightning flashed every few seconds. Galin somehow seemed to anticipate each strike, keeping us in the shadows, out of sight of the lupine predators. But I could see them now, their hairy forms everywhere as we raced between buildings. It was only a matter of time before they spotted us.

A howl tore through the air, so close it made the ground rumble.

They were closing in on us.

CHAPTER 20

ALI

We were nearly at Bilskirnir, the towering castle of the gods. Three blocks away now. My breath rasped in my throat as I ran in an all-out sprint, on a narrow street that took us between crumbling buildings.

As I moved, my gaze swept up the length of the castle. The first few hundred feet were pure stone, but after that small windows dotted the walls, dark and empty. If anyone, or thing, lived within the marble edifice, it was impossible to tell from outside.

"Is there an entrance?" I gasped.

"I hope so."

Galin, you need to learn to be more reassuring.

I rushed after him all the same, running down a particularly narrow alley. Then lightning flashed directly in front of us, so bright it completely blinded me.

When my vision cleared again, fear slithered up my spine, and I skidded to a halt. A massive shadow moved in front of Galin, glowing yellow eyes beaming in the darkness.

Galin slowed, raising his hand to scribe. But the dragon blood had left his voice raspy, barely audible. And before he could finish, the wolf lunged, its huge maw gaping open, ready to snap shut like a bear trap.

Galin dodged just in time, but the wolf was already crouching, preparing to spring.

"Skalei," I whispered. The hilt of my knife was in my hand, and I threw it hard. It spun into the wolf's eye.

The wolf leapt back. With a mewling cry, it turned and bounded off into the darkness.

Galin whirled, shock etched on his features.

I exhaled. "Been practicing more than just spells."

Galin opened his mouth to speak, but he couldn't seem to raise his voice above a whisper. And that meant he wouldn't be doing powerful magic anytime soon. Fear began to claw at me. If Galin couldn't scribe a portal, and we were being hunted by giant wolves, we had no margin for error.

"Let's go," I whispered. "Skalei."

With my blade in my hand, we started running again.

We cut through the rubble of a ruined building, heading for the next street. Howls cut through the air, making the stones tremble, and Galin pulled me into a doorway. Just in time—two massive wolves bounded past, eyes glowing in the dark.

"They can't smell us because of the rain," Galin whispered.

With the wolves past, we crept out again, more slowly now. The rain fell in ice-cold sheets, hammering my skin. My clothes were saturated, and I started to shiver.

A deep growl trembled over the horizon, rumbling across the ruins.

Galin pulled us into another doorway. Rainwater slid down his tattooed chest in little rivulets.

"Ali," he rasped. "You need to scribe a portal. My voice isn't working well enough for the spell. You did it before.

When the troll—" He winced, falling silent, eyes closed. Clearly it hurt him to speak. "I'll help with the rune."

I sucked in a deep breath. "Okay."

Galin slipped behind me, his powerful body pressed against mine. Warmth radiated over me from his chest, and he slid his hand down my arm, sending a hot shiver through my body.

Distracting. If he wanted me to focus on the spell, he would need to stop distracting me.

I extended my arm, pointing my finger—ready to scribe the spell. Galin's hand wrapped around mine, helping to perfect the shape of the runes. His smoky, masculine scent wrapped around my body like a caress, and I could feel his magic thrumming over my skin. My back arched, breath quickening.

Love. I need to think of love.

As my hand moved, I concentrated on my voice, on the incantation, on the *feeling* of love. Before, when I was hanging on the ladder on the side of Mount Steton, I hadn't had time to think of a particular moment, a time when my heart had felt full. I just did it. Somehow, it came from me.

But now, I tried to remember what Galin had told me. How he'd explained that he always thought of his mother—the love grief had revealed to him after her death. I tried to think of my own mom, but it had been so long ago. And I could mostly only remember her sick, on her death bed. I'd been so little. I couldn't even remember her face anymore.

A wolf howled. So close and loud I could feel my lungs vibrate in my chest. Whatever sense of love I might have found was replaced with blinding terror.

Love.

A hundred yards down the street, a massive wolf strode into view—nearly three stories tall, with dark matted fur and long legs. It sniffed at the ground, then lifted its head and howled.

Galin tried to speak, but it only came out in a whisper again. "Run."

We broke into a sprint, tearing down the street away from the wolf.

We swerved sharply left, and Galin gestured to a broken window. I leapt in, narrowly avoiding the jagged glass. Galin was right behind me.

The wolf tore past us, giant toenails clacking loudly on the marble. We ran again, rushing through the interiors of the abandoned buildings, leaping over piles of broken marble, ducking under shattered beams.

All around us, a frenzy of howling boomed through the city, deafening. Wolves in a full chorus of hunting cries. Hungry for our flesh. It seemed like they'd surrounded us now.

When we got to the end of the block, I saw that at last, we'd reached the great wall of the castle, built of marble blocks twenty feet high.

Unfortunately there was no sign of any sort of doorway.

My lungs heaved as I looked to Galin.

"What now?" I mouthed.

He nodded at the pack of wolves, and an understanding dawned. They were guarding the entrance.

There was no other way in.

Moving more slowly now, we began to make our way towards them, using the castle wall to protect our right flank, keeping our eyes fixed on the streets to our left. Looking for any sign of movement. As we reached a particularly large and open boulevard, I saw a giant set of doors carved into marble, a hundred yards off. Above it, a string of runes was written on the stone. Unfortunately, I couldn't read them from here.

We crept closer, and fear clutched at me again. Filling the entire end of the boulevard and blocking the doors was an enormous wolf—jet black fur and big green eyes that gleamed in the darkness. The largest wolf I'd seen yet.

My heart skipped a beat as the beast's head swung in our direction, and I realized it'd spotted us. For a moment its green eyes fixed on mine, then it raised its massive head and howled.

Across the boulevard was a clattering of rubble as two more wolves strode into view. The fear that had been percolating in my veins began to curdle.

"Skalei."

Side by side, Galin and I moved into the boulevard, away from the wolves. I gripped Skalei tightly.

Then the black wolf barked, and another pair of wolves appeared, cutting off our retreat.

Galin moved round behind me, so that we stood back to back. Prowling, the wolves closed in on us—two facing me, two facing Galin. The big black alpha continued to watch from the steps of the castle.

The rain slowed, and the wet stones of the boulevard shone with moonlight. Across from me, the pair of wolves stalked closer, icy mist swirling around their forepaws.

I threw Skalei, and the blade flashed in the moonlight. It was a good throw, but as the blade neared, the wolf jerked its head to the side and Skalei flashed past, clattering harmlessly on the stones.

Balls.

"Skalei."

Behind me, Galin tried to speak, but all that came out was a faint rasping sound.

My jaw clenched. *Of all the times to lose his ability to speak properly ...*

But if I couldn't summon love—what about anger? I

dropped Skalei and raised my right hand. As fast as I could, I began to scribe *kaun*.

The pair of wolves across from me crouched, ready to jump. Anticipatory drool dripped from their jaws. In moments they'd be upon us. We'd be torn to shreds.

I gritted my teeth, letting rage build within me. I hadn't come this far to end up as dog food. I was Ali, daughter of Volundar. I was an Empress, ruler of all elves. And I could do magic.

The anger was white hot within me. Churning in my veins like molten lava. Galin pressed his back against mine. His muscles rock hard, his shoulders completely rigid. I could feel his sympathetic rage. The anger that was simultaneously boiling his blood, feeding mine. He must have sensed what I was doing, and he was helping me somehow.

I slashed the final rune through the air, as I spat out the last syllable of the spell.

My rage, Galin's rage, every ounce of anger I could possibly summon, I channeled into the rune. Just as one of the wolves started to pounce, the air around us began to shimmer. Then, with a blast of heat, the air exploded in an incandescent inferno. Heat burst from my body, and flames raced out in all directions like the shockwave of a meteor strike. The wolves yelped with pain as they leapt away, racing into the rubble of the broken city, fur blazing.

And then the spell was done, and my legs gave out. Weak, shaking, I slid down Galin's back. My vision narrowed to a single point, but Galin's powerful arms were around me.

With one arm supporting my back and the other under my knees, he lifted me to his bare chest. I looked up into his perfect features, his pitch-black eyes reflecting the stars above.

Then my vision flickered, as Galin turned to face

Bilskirnir. The castle doors appeared above us, carved with the faces of the gods—and a single word. *Valhalla.*

CHAPTER 21

ALI

Galin held me against his wet, bare chest as he carried me inside. Fatigue shattered my body, making my muscles shake. The fire spell had wrecked me.

Inside Valhalla, darkness enveloped us. Galin of course couldn't see a thing, nor with his wrecked voice could he call up a spell for light. I would have to be his eyes.

Still, even before my eyes adjusted I knew something was off. It smelled of smoke and old food, as if someone was living here.

I squinted until the room came into focus. I saw the marble first. There were stairs at one end, and long hallways in either direction. Detritus lay in heaps all over the place—gnawed bones, old ragged clothing, and a charred pile of logs in the center.

"Galin," I whispered, "we're in some sort of entrance hall. There are bones everywhere, but I don't see anyone around."

Galin grunted something unintelligible, then gently set me down on the floor. My muscles still felt like rubber bands, but I'd gained enough body control to lean against the doors. I was exhausted, still soaking wet. Galin slouched next to me, and I found myself leaning against his bare chest, which was like pure steel under his smooth skin. Warm, though.

Shadow magic swirled about his skin, whispering over my cold body with tingles that raised goosebumps. Then, he turned to open the doors to the city of Asgard.

"Where are you going?" I asked. But Galin had already disappeared back into the ruined city, the door creaking shut behind him.

Alone, I turned back to the interior. In the darkness, it just looked like blank marble, featureless walls. No sign of any windows, just a massive atrium with a ceiling so high it was obscured by darkness. The air was completely still. After the deafening howling of the wolves, it was strange to be in a place so quiet.

Then the golden doors creaked open, and Galin appeared, holding a chunk of burning lumber—a crude torch.

"Can you walk?" he whispered.

"I'm not sure." I tried to take a few steps, but immediately my legs gave out.

Galin's arm swept out, slipping around my waist to stop me from falling.

I leaned into him. "If you help hold me up I think I can walk." With Galin's arm tight around my waist, I was able to support my remaining weight. Slowly, we staggered forward.

"The magic wrecked me," I said quietly.

Supporting me with one arm, holding the torch with the other, Galin helped me cross the hall. He paused at the stairs, looking at me with a questioning expression.

"I can do it," I assured him.

One step at a time, we began to climb. Slowly, we ascended to the second level, then the third. Light from his torch danced over the hall, shadows wavering over marble.

By the fourth-floor landing, I heard a noise that nearly made me stumble: the unmistakable whining of a wolf.

"I thought I killed them," I said as Galin dragged me into the shadows, away from the stairwell. "Guess I need more fire next time."

I pressed in close to him, waiting to see if the wolf would enter the castle. But we only heard whining, scratching, thumping. Apparently they couldn't open doors.

Galin held up a finger, then disappeared into the darkness of one of the halls.

Freaking Hel. His lack of speech was not the best situation, because I had no idea what was going on.

Again, I was left to wait in the darkness, slumped against a wall. The cold from the rain had gone right down to my marrow, which made my muscles more rigid. I tried to walk again, but my legs were still too weak. I wanted to know how to do magic without destroying my strength, without making myself useless.

I slid down the wall to rest. My teeth chattered, fingers frozen. When I exhaled, my breath misted around me. As I was massaging my thighs, I saw his silhouette moving through the shadows.

Galin—for once—was smiling broadly.

"What is it?" I asked.

Instead of answering, he crouched down and helped me up, arm protectively around my waist. With his help, I hobbled along the balcony away from the stairwell. From here, I could see the marble floor four stories below us, the fire pit, and the gleam of the golden doors.

Galin turned and pushed open a door. I gasped at the beauty of the room beyond. Now *this* looked like how I'd imagined Valhalla.

A set of windows illuminated the interior in cool moonlight. This place was not only clean, but it looked comfortable. Oak walls engraved with swirls, a soft rug on the floor, a large four-poster bed.

But most of all, my eyes were drawn to the fireplace—an enormous stone hearth inset into oak walls. A fire burned within it. I nearly cried as I felt its heat wash over me.

As we approached, I took in the piles of pillows on the floor—soft and golden. I was ready to collapse into them, but Galin held me up.

"I want to sleep there," I whispered.

But he shook his head quickly, a clear *No*.

Then he began to pull my wet leather jacket off me, and it fell to the floor with a wet thunk.

My shirt had soaked through too.

What had Galin said to me? He felt nothing for me. Since I'd severed the mating bond, he didn't feel a thing at all.

He was supposed to be dead inside, right?

Something naughty stirred in me, and I wanted to see whether or not that was true. And what better time than when icy rainwater soaked me down to my bones?

With a smile, I reached down and pulled off my shirt, then threw it on the floor. I followed his gaze down to my red lacy bra, enjoying the widening of his eyes. The effect of the ice-cold rain on my nipples was clearly apparent to him. He'd gone still as the ancient statues outside. For just a moment, his hand reached out for my waist. Then his fist tightened, and he pulled his hand away.

This was delightful.

I cocked my head. "I'll need help out of my pants. They're soaked. You were very clear that you don't feel any desire, so it shouldn't be a problem, right?"

When he met my gaze, the look was searing, piercing me down to my very soul. I guessed he did feel something—yet he didn't seem to want to admit it.

I stepped closer, making my eyes wide and innocent. "You don't want me to be cold, do you? Like you said. You don't feel desire, so what's the issue?"

I unbuttoned the top of my pants, then brought his hands to my waist. With the faintest of smiles, he pulled the pants off me—a little too fast, like he was annoyed I was calling his bluff.

He helped me step out of them, then started to rise again, his eyes tracing up my bare thighs, lingering on my little red panties—bright against my pale skin.

I pouted at him. "I'll need help getting to the pillow, my desires-less friend. Good thing you won't be distracted by lust or anything." Was I laying it on too thick? I had to take my fun where I could get it these days.

A muscle twitched in his jaw, and all the muscles in his chest had gone completely rigid while he looked at my half-naked body.

Then he stepped forward, scooped me up, and lay me down across the pillows, in the warmth of the fire.

I almost reached for him, but I forced myself to stop. If he wanted me, he was going to have to admit it.

I watched as he crossed to the bed and pulled off a heavy blanket for me. He lay it over me, and I pulled it up around my chin.

I felt warm, inside and out, the heat of the fire warming my cheek. My muscles were so tired I was virtually paralyzed, but for the first time in ages, I felt entirely at peace.

I glanced at Galin, now spreading my clothes out to dry. He looked nearly as exhausted as myself.

I realized now why he'd been smiling so excitedly when he came back to me in the hallway. Just as I did, when he first entered the room, he must have immediately seen the fireplace. He'd made a fire, then come back for me.

Maybe I felt a *little* bit bad for teasing him.

Galin settled in an armchair, still shirtless, black vapor rising from his tattoos, his eyes focused on the fire. It was obvious he was a powerful sorcerer, but I knew something no one else in the nine worlds knew.

Deep down, he was kind of sweet.

Galin saw me looking at him, and met my gaze for so long I wondered if I should look away again. Then, he spoke in a rough whisper. "In the morning, we'll search for the well. Nice throw with Skalei."

"I've been practicing," I murmured.

I leaned back again against the pillow, my eyelids growing heavy. I closed my eyes, listening to the logs crackling in the fire, the wind rattling the windows, and something more.

A distant howling. Fenrir's children were out there somewhere, licking their wounds.

CHAPTER 22

ALI

I don't know how long I slept—only that when I woke, Galin was gone. But why did I wake up? Outside it was nearly pitch black; the moon must have gone behind a cloud. The fire that had lit the room earlier was now nearly out. Only a faint glow of embers shone in the fireplace.

Where is Galin? And what just woke me?

Then I heard it: a distant shout. Too high pitched to be a wolf's or a man's.

A woman was in here somewhere.

As I tried to work out what was going on, there was another shout.

"Oi, Gondul!"

A pause, followed by feminine laughter. Not a single voice, but at least four or five women.

"Gawn-dull!"

"Shut up Hildr," snapped a second voice.

"Gondul why are you such a nasty troll?"

"Hildr, I'm not in the mood."

"Gods be damned, you nearly knocked me off my horse."

What on earth was going on? Who were these women nattering on in the night? And where the Hel was Galin?

I pushed myself up onto my elbows, relieved to discover that sleep had washed away much of the paralyzing exhaustion. Climbing slowly to my feet, I hunched-walked to the door and pressed an ear against it.

Through the oak, I could hear the rest of the women talking and laughing, though I couldn't understand what they were saying. I felt like a kid in her bedroom, listening to her parents hosting a dinner party. I supposed we had barged in here, and clearly people lived in this place. These must be the ones littering the floor with gnawed bones.

Gondul's voice cracked through the wood like a gunshot. "You need to shoulder your spear properly."

"You know I pulled a muscle last week."

"Oh don't make stuff up, you know you can't get injured. And I saw you drinking from your horn. That's probably why you can't get your spear up. Flaccid weapon. Absolutely useless."

The other woman laughed uproariously at Gondul's joke, and I just barely heard Hildr's reply. "The mead gives me strength."

Doors slammed. Dogs barked. Someone shouted, "Shut the Hel up, you stupid mutts." Followed by loud muttering, "Gods, the damn dogs won't stop yapping. What's gotten into them?"

"Hildr, shut the darn door, you know Fenrir's pups don't listen," yelled Gondul.

"Who's got the mead?" someone cried out.

"Here," replied another voice.

A long pause followed, then, "Gods, it warms my tits."

The women crowed with laughter. "Were your tits cold?" The laughter increased in volume, then someone shouted, "Hildr's tits are pure ice."

I was thinking about trying to slip out of the room and take a peek over the railing when I heard Gondul shout, "Pipe down yah old hags, I'm trying to enjoy my stew."

Someone jeered. "Stew! Bet you'd like some sausage in that stew of yours. Been a while, hasn't it?"

"Shut up, Hildr," said Gondul. "I don't need reminding."

But at this point Hildr was not stopping. "Big meaty sausage! Something you can really get your mouth around," she shouted, her voice slurring. The rest of the women howled with glee.

At that moment, the door pushed open, and Galin slipped into the room.

"Galin," I whispered. "What the fuck is going on?"

"Valkyries."

"Whoa … That's what valkyries sound like?"

"Yup," Galin whispered. "I saw them when I was exploring. They flew in on their winged horses a little while ago."

"What are we going to do?" I asked.

"Just sit tight, I'll go talk to them. They seem … jolly."

I wasn't sure this was a good idea, but before I could reply, Galin was gone. Below, the valkyries suddenly went silent.

"Who are you?" barked one of them.

"Galin—"

"Look at that beauty! The abs on him …"

Galin tried to say something, but another valkyrie cut him off. "I get him first. You see those sharp muscles near his groin? Those are sex lines."

There was more shouting.

Then Galin spoke, his voice rasping. "Valkyries, I am Galin, King of Hel, consort to the goddess Hela—"

"Gods damn. Hela's not going to let us fuck him, is she? But his mouth is so pretty. I want his mouth on me."

"What if it's just for a few minutes?" someone cried.

"Don't listen to Hildr. She'll want it again and again. Up against the wall, tied up. Can you just take your trousers off, though? It has been *ages.* I want to see it. Now."

The valkyries lost it at this point, literally screaming and shrieking. I got the impression they had already consumed quite a lot of mead.

"Valkyries!" said Galin again, trying to get things under control. "I am here on a quest—" But his broken voice just wasn't up to the task of reining in the intoxicated valkyries.

"I just want your pretty mouth on me, though!"

"Face it, Hildr, he's not gonna lick your muff, is he?"

At this point I decided that weak legs or not, I needed to come to Galin's rescue. I pushed the door open and staggered to the edge of the balcony.

Looking down, I saw Galin standing in the center of the castle atrium, surrounded. Warm firelight danced over six statuesque women dressed in gleaming silver armor over white dresses. They looked beautiful and athletic—and were grinning like drunken maniacs. Most of them held drinking horns.

"Hey," I shouted. "Stop asking him to take his pants off. It's not on."

They spun round to look at me, eyes furious, piercing.

Galin might be welcome here, but I was not.

"Is that Hela?" someone slurred.

"No, you idiot," said the largest valkyrie, in Gondul's voice. "Hela died, remember? That's just a little Night Elf—"

Galin managed to cut in then, "This is my companion, Astrid Volundar, Empress of the Vanir—"

"That little wench is an empress? I could break her in two with my bare hands."

"Galin speaks the truth," I said as firmly as I could. "I am Empress of the Vanir, leader of—"

"Oh fuck off, she's hardly more than a speck of a thing.

This man needs a *real* woman," shouted one of the valkyries. "Hildr, take off your dress."

"He doesn't feel desire!" I called out. "It's a whole thing."

"When he gets a peek at those frozen tits of Hildr's, he'll raise his blade. She could cut glass with her nipples, you know. Carve the whole Poetic Edda in a window."

This induced paroxysms of laughter, as the valkyries stumbled around, gulping mead from their drinking horns and repeating the phrase, "Raise his blade! Raise his blade!"

I could not decide if I loved them or hated them.

"Ok, I'll do it," shouted Hildr suddenly, and she began to fumble with her armor. "I'll have a crack at that beautiful mouth. And the sex lines."

The valkyries cheered, throwing their mead into the air.

"That's it Hildr, give him a peek at your thatched cottage!" shouted a valkyrie who appeared barely able to stand.

"Let him taste your plum tree," goaded another.

As Hildr stumbled around trying to unclasp her sword belt, another valkyrie began chanting, "Bugle-hole, Bugle-hole!" for no apparent reason. I wasn't sure I wanted to know what that was.

"Quiet," shouted the most somber of the valkyries.

Of course Hildr ignored her, and her armor clattered to the floor. "Almost got 'em out ladies," she yelled excitedly, while almost tripping over her sword belt. "Nothing you all haven't seen before, but I'll get his dagger stiff."

But before Hildr could make further progress towards removing her dress, Gondul suddenly drew her sword. With a lightning-fast strike, she plunged it through Hildr's neck. Hildr fell to the floor with a gurgling shriek, blood pouring from her throat.

Dread stopped my heart. Holy shit. These women were insane.

The valkyries fell silent—until Hildr crawled to her

knees, coughing and spitting blood. For a moment I couldn't believe what I was seeing. Her neck had nearly been severed.

In my shock, I'd nearly forgotten that valkyries couldn't die.

"Gods in Hel Gondul, you know that's *not* the kind of dagger I was talking about," Hildr yelled as her neck healed. "It's a euphemism for his penis."

"I understood the metaphor." Gondul glared at Hildr.

I half expected Hildr to draw her own sword and fight the valkyrie leader, but instead she snatched a mead horn from a valkyrie standing next to her and began to drink loudly from it.

"Are you quite done?" Gondul barked.

Hildr threw the horn on the ground. "You know it really parches my throat when you stab me in the neck. I'm just having a little fun with our guest, right girls?"

"Valkyries," said Galin again, trying to gain control of the situation. "I am here on a quest. I need your help—"

"Why should we help you?" Gondul snapped.

"I'm looking for information. I'm interested in visiting Mimisbrunnr. We would be most appreciative if you could show us where it is."

Gondul shook her head, her blonde hair cascading over her silver epaulets. "We don't do anything without payment."

Galin frowned. "I don't have any money."

"I wasn't speaking of money."

Galin's body went tense. "I'm not bartering my body."

"So I've gathered," said Gondul. "How 'bout the little princess then? Maybe she can offer us something. Doesn't have to be money."

"What do you propose?"

"How 'bout if she wins a fight with my best warrior, I'll help you find Mimisbrunnr."

"And if I lose?" I cut in, not liking where this was going.

An enormous grin spread across Gondul's face. "If you lose, Hildr, myself, and the rest of us valkyries get a little taste of that dagger of his."

"Absolutely not," I began.

"On one condition," said Galin, cutting me off.

"Galin!" I shouted, "What are you doing?"

But Gondul held up a hand. "And what would that be?"

"I choose the contest and the fighter."

Gondul shook her head. "You choose the contest, I choose the fighter."

What the fuck was he getting me into?

Before I had a chance to negotiate, Galin nodded his assent. "Deal."

CHAPTER 23

ALI

"Galin," I hissed as I stumbled down the last few steps to the atrium. "I'm not sure this is a good idea."

Only when his gaze swept over me did I remember I was still half naked. I wasn't sure the valkyries would care either way.

"You'll fight with your dagger. You'll win handily."

I glared at him. "No, I won't. I can barely stand. I can't believe you thought this was a good idea."

Galin's eyes widened. "You still haven't recovered?"

I nodded hard.

"Maybe we should try to escape?" he whispered. "I think I can cast a portal now. My voice is coming back."

I looked to the six massive valkyries watching us—and the one who stepped forward, ready to fight me with her dagger. "I nominate myself to fight the tiny elf."

Gondul was nearly as tall as Galin, her arms cut with muscle, shoulders broad. She was beautiful, but she also looked like she could crush my skull. And the cold fury in her eyes suggested that that was exactly what she was thinking about. If we fled, I was pretty sure she and the rest of the valkyries would hunt us to the ends of the earth.

And worst of all, we wouldn't be able to finish our quest.

I shook my head. "No, we need to find Mimisbrunnr. I don't think Gondul will accept anything but a fight at this point. You saw what she did to Hildr. The important thing is that Midgard and Vanaheim are not overrun by the draugr hordes."

"You think you can do it?" he asked.

I took a shaky breath. "I'm going to give it my best shot."

His black eyes searched mine. "You will not die. I promise."

My fingers twitched, as cockiness started to bubble in my chest. "I know. I'm not going to let her kill me. Don't worry about it."

Galin turned back to the valkyries. "Here are the rules. First one to draw the other's blood three times wins. Does that seem fair?"

"Yes." Gondul's eyes flicked to Skalei. "But no magic. Just blades."

While the rest of the valkyries backed up to give us room, I spoke to Gondul. "You're wearing armor. I'll just get dressed."

"No clothing." Her voice boomed over the hall, and she started pulling off her armor. "If we are to see a scratch on the skin then we must fight in our underwear. You can stay as you are, princess."

Empress.

I stared as she pulled off her dress, revealing a pair of underwear that looked like little shorts—but nothing on top. I supposed valkyries didn't wear bras. A thick blonde braid fell over her heavily muscled shoulders.

I held up my right hand, then called Skalei.

Gondul's eyebrows flicked up ever so slightly as the blade appeared in my grip.

She smiled wickedly, blue eyes flashing, her teeth white as

snow. Then, crouching down, she drew a long silver dagger from her boot. The thing was massive, practically a sword compared to Skalei.

"Oi! She's the size of a child," cackled Hildr. "Gondul, don't break the wee one."

"Are you ready?" asked Galin.

Gondul nodded.

"All right." Galin's voice was clearer now, and he raised his hands above his head. "In three, two, one." A pause, then he dropped his hands. "Fight!"

The valkyries began cheering as Gondul tossed her blonde braid over her shoulder and began to stalk towards me.

"You ready to feel the steel of my blade, little one?"

I backed away, testing my legs. They were definitely unsteady.

"You can't run from me, princess."

"I'm not a princess."

Gondul laughed, still moving towards me. "Whatever you are, you should brace yourself for pain."

She lunged fast, but I'd anticipated it and willed my legs into action. Somehow I managed to leap to the side while slashing up with Skalei. As Gondul passed, I felt the blade slice her skin.

The valkyrie spun on her heels, blood dripping from her shoulder, eyes blazing with excitement. "Not bad, princess. The first hit."

Galin stepped forward. "We must check the wound."

Gondul slowed, then stopped as Galin and the valkyries crowded round. Panting, my hands on my knees, I watched them check the cut on her shoulder.

"Gods in Hel, Gondul," swore Hildr, looking extremely put out. "You've got to win this. I haven't had a chance with a bloke in ages, you know."

"Don't be ridiculous," hissed Gondul. "Of course I've got this."

Galin and the valkyries stepped back.

"Then the score is settled: one to zero. The Empress leads," Galin declared.

I gripped Skalei, trying not to get too complacent. I still had to cut the massive valkyrie two more times, and it wasn't going to get any easier. In the next round, Gondul would be more cautious, more cunning, and I was at a serious disadvantage with my tired legs.

We squared off again, twenty feet apart. Gondul held her dagger tightly in her right hand, her legs slightly apart, her ice-blue eyes fiercely focused on me.

Galin stood between us. "Round two, in three, two, one" —a millisecond pause—"fight!"

Gondul lunged. I'd expected her to be more careful this time, to force me to attack. Instead, the powerful woman barreled towards me like a wrecking ball.

I braced myself, gripping Skalei. Was she going to do the same thing again? She'd already seen what happened with this approach. All I had to do was leap out of the way, and slash with my blade.

As she moved closer, I dodged to the left, away from her blade hand. I slashed with Skalei—but this was not the same attack.

She swung at my head with her free hand. I tried to duck, but the valkyrie was experienced, and her fist slammed into my temple with a crunch. Stars filled my vision, and my legs gave out.

I hadn't even hit the floor when Gondul's dagger plunged into my chest. Ice-cold steel pierced my heart, a blow so hard it sent me slamming into the marble. Gondul followed, leaping on me. Straddling me, she tore out the blade and raised it victoriously above her head, shrieking like a banshee. A numbing chill had filled my core, and along with it—panic.

This had been her plan all along. She never intended on using her blade to scratch or mark me. She'd gone straight for the kill.

I coughed, spitting up hot blood. The panic started to leave me.

I'd always assumed that death would be painful. That I'd writhe and moan, fight till the very end. But all I felt was cold spreading through me, ice in my veins. The marble was cool against my back, the sounds of the valkyries soft and distant. My vision flickered as if I were about to fall asleep.

But I didn't entirely welcome the end. No, a dull fury was coursing through me. There was so much I'd left unfinished. The draugr horde still threatened my people; Barthol remained trapped in Hel. Even Galin deserved a better fate. I looked to him, a blurry form above me. Regret ripped me open. He was no longer my mate—but the thought of leaving him was agony.

He was talking to me, but the words were lost to me now.

I shut my eyes. A true warrior dies in battle.

CHAPTER 24

ALI

My heart twitched. Lurched hard in my chest. Beat once, twice, a third time. My lungs convulsed. I coughed hot blood onto the marble.

"What is going on? Am I dead?" I managed to croak before spitting up more blood.

Gondul flashed me a smug grin. "Before Ragnarok, the greatest warriors lived here. We'd fight all day, then drink and fuck all night. In Valhalla you cannot die. Here, you are like us."

Of course, she is right. That was why Galin had said I wouldn't die. He meant it literally.

Galin reached down and helped me to my feet. I leaned against him, clutching my chest. My skin burned where Gondul's dagger had penetrated it.

"Hurts though, doesn't it. Never gets easier." She passed me her drinking horn. "Apart from the fear. That goes away. Mead helps."

I waved it away, wanting to stay alert. "No thank you."

Gondul smiled. "You may be tiny, but you're not stupid. Smart to keep your wits about you. Ready for the third round?"

I definitely was not ready. My legs were jelly, my chest throbbed, my mouth still tasted of blood. But I didn't get the sense the valkyries would let me wait around till I felt up to it.

I nodded to Galin. "Any time."

Tentatively, he stepped away from me, then quickly counted down.

This time Gondul didn't charge.

"Your turn princess," she said quietly, her blue eyes flashing. Goading me.

"I am not a princess."

I stalked forward, or at least I tried to; my legs were still unsteady.

"Gondul!" shouted Hildr. "The little bird's got a lame wing. Put her out of her misery."

Gondul grunted, her eyes narrowing predatorily. She began to circle me, passing her dagger back and forth between her hands, showing off.

I moved with her, keeping distance. Waiting.

"You can't run from me," growled Gondul.

I needed her to strike first. My only chance was to counterattack.

What had Hildr said? *Bird's got a lame wing.* I remembered how Swegde had once pointed out a little bird in the grasslands. "That's a killdeer," he explained. "They lay their eggs in the grass. No nest. But if you get too close, they pretend to be hurt. The predator chases them and they lead them away from their babies."

I could use that—feign a worse injury and lure Gondul in close enough to strike.

Clutching my heart, I staggered. I pretended to trip over the stones. Gondul stepped forward, gripping her knife tightly.

As I pretended to fall, I hurled Skalei. The blade glinted in the firelight.

I'd aimed for Gondul's throat, but at the last moment she tried to twist out of the way, and the blade hit her in the ribs, between her breasts. She fell back, eyes bulging as she clutched her chest, Skalei's hilt protruding through her fingertips.

"Nearly ruined your tits!" Hildr called out.

Gondul's face contorted, and she ripped out Skalei, hurling it across the room. It lodged in the marble ten feet above my head.

"That's two marks for Ali, one for Gondul," said Galin.

The huge valkyrie glared at me, blood pouring down her chest. She looked furious now, her grip so tight on her dagger the blade shook. She didn't like to lose.

I opened my mouth to call for my blade, but Gondul cut me off as she bellowed, "No magic."

She didn't wait for Galin to count off the round. She just charged. Screaming at the top of her lungs, she barreled towards me like an enraged rhinoceros, her dagger held straight out. I tried to dodge, but my legs still felt like lead. My heart beat like a war drum, adrenalin sparking through my nerves.

In my mind's eye, I saw what came next. Gondul stabbing as I flailed, her dagger on an unerring path to my heart, the searing pain as the blade severed my aorta.

Gondul was almost upon me, her dagger slicing downward like a viper's tooth. But I wasn't about to let myself be stabbed in the chest again. I threw up my right arm. Gondul's blade plunged through my forearm, as her momentum carried her into me. She drove me back, my arm above my head.

I lost my footing then, instinctively grabbing the only thing I could reach—Gondul's wrist. The mighty valkyrie's inertia continued to carry me backward, until we fell with a crash. I hit the marble hard, and Gondul fell on top of me. Blinding pain lanced through my arm, and I screamed as the valkyrie's dagger wrenched awkwardly, digging into my bone.

I expected Gondul to rear back, to howl in victory, but instead the beast of a woman lay on top of me like a blanket of muscle. I tried to move, but the valkyrie wouldn't budge.

"Let me up," I gasped. "You won that round."

Gondul didn't move. Blood dripped down my arm, and I struggled to breathe.

"Gondul, stop playing around!" shouted Hildr. "She's a princess, not a mattress."

Only then did the massive valkyrie's body shift, rolling off me at last. I gasped as pain radiated down my arm. Even without looking, I knew that Gondul's dagger was still embedded in it.

Then a shadow passed over me, and I saw Galin's black eyes looking down. "Are you okay?"

"I'm fine. Dagger's still in my arm, right?"

With a grimace, Galin nodded. Behind him I saw the valkyries peer at me.

Hildr's eyebrows flicked up, and her eyes flashed with excitement. "Girls, Gondul got her in the forearm, it's two to two! One final round to decide it!" She wiggled her hips. "And then the fun begins."

It was as I'd expected. One last fight. Everything on the line. I needed to get up and somehow collect my blade, lodged several feet above my head. *Gods, this isn't good.*

But Galin didn't seem worried. "Hildr, I believe you're mistaken." He pointed to Gondul. The valkyrie lay on the floor, flat on her back, her eyes unfocused. My blood stained the skin of her chest. Galin pointed to her neck.

I sucked in a short breath. Along the side of her throat, a

deep wound was bleeding. Simultaneously, the other valkyries and I realized its significance. When Gondul slammed me to the floor, her own blade, lodged as it was in my arm, had sliced open her throat. She hadn't been lying on top of me as some sort of act of dominance. She'd been dead.

Gondul's eyes snapped open. "What's going on?"

There was a long pause as the valkyries simply glared at her. At last Hildr spoke. "You ruined our chances of getting laid, you stupid cow."

"What?" said Gondul, in complete disbelief.

"You fell on your own blade." Hildr held up three fingers, then two. "Three marks for her, only two for you."

"Gods damned!" shouted Gondul, slamming her fist against the floor. "Gods damned. That tiny thing?"

The valkyries stood with eyes downcast, obviously disappointed. Hildr looked like she might cry. I couldn't say I felt very sorry for them.

"Give me your hand," said Galin. I thought he was going to help me up, but instead he yanked out Gondul's dagger.

I clenched my jaw as pain shot up my arm like a lightning bolt. And yet, with the magic of Valhalla, I could already feel it healing.

Galin pulled me up properly and I glared at him. "Next time, let's find a solution that doesn't involve me getting stabbed."

He pinned me with his gaze. "I knew you would win. Now, we still have business with the valkyries. Gondul has a promise to keep."

CHAPTER 25

ALI

Galin turned back to Gondul and the valkyries. "Tell us how to get to Mimisbrunnr."

Gondul laughed. "I don't know where the Hel that place is."

Dark shadows swirled around Galin. He seemed to grow larger, air darkening around him, and a chill rippled over me. Gondul might be scary, but Galin was scarier. "You gave your word."

"I told you I'd *help* you find it."

"All right," said Galin slowly, "then help us."

* * *

I DRESSED AGAIN, in clothes that were still damp, and waited for Gondul and Galin outside the room I would have liked to curl up in for a nap. My body felt shattered, but it looked like we were moving again. Even if the pillows were more inviting than anything.

Gondul arrived, wearing her clothes and armor again. There was a bit of blood in her hair, but otherwise she looked completely healed. I leaned against the doorway, trying to ignore the pain in my body.

"Why is it that I'm so tired and Galin's throat is still injured?" I asked. "And yet I've recovered from being stabbed in the heart?"

Gondul shrugged. "Only injuries sustained in Valhalla heal. If you hurt yourself outside these walls, the magic doesn't help. I hope you're up for climbing stairs."

Not really. I plastered a smile on my face.

Gondul turned away and started up. I tightened my fists as I followed.

But as soon as her back was turned, I leaned on Galin. My legs shuddered as we climbed, my arm wrapped around his bare waist. We didn't speak—Galin still hoarse, and me too tired.

"Where are you taking us?" asked Galin.

"You'll see," Gondul called out. "Where is your sense of adventure?"

Flight after flight, ascending toward the skies.

We'd been climbing for what seemed like hours—though it might have been thirty minutes—when Gondul turned off one of the landings. We followed her down a long hallway. Torches lit sleek ivory marble. At the end of the hall, we reached a set of dark mahogany doors carved with ravens. A shiver ran over me, the feeling of a long-dormant power rippling over the stone.

Gondul turned to us. "These were once Odin's quarters." Then, she opened the doors.

I gasped. Inside was a breathtaking apartment. A row of windows along one wall revealed a panoramic view of Asgard. The city was a shattered ruin, but even so it was spectacular—shimmering stone in silver light spread out before us.

Paintings on the walls depicted great scenes of battle,

boats sailing across the sea—and ravens, everywhere. Here, in a god's quarters, I felt like I was trespassing.

Gondul waltzed in as if she owned the place, sauntering over to a side room.

With Galin's help, I followed. An enormous bed stood in the middle of the room, draped with fur blankets.

I glanced at Galin. What did he think about exploring a god's personal chambers? The expression of near horror on his face succinctly answered the question.

Gondul dropped to the floor and began rummaging under the bed. I couldn't imagine what she could be looking for, until she pulled out a small alligator skin case.

"This should answer your questions." She placed it onto the bed.

Galin frowned. "What is it? You have taken something from Odin?"

Gondul tossed her braid behind her shoulder. "Open it. Where is your sense of adventure?"

Galin stared at the case for a long minute. Then, in a swift and fluid move, he unclasped the lid. As he did, a horrible shriek filled the room. Galin stepped back, shielding me with his arm.

It took me one horrifying moment to realize what it was—a severed head, matted with blood, shrieking into the air.

What the *fuck*?

"Is this some sort of joke?" I said. Was this what Odin had become?

"No," said Galin. He leaned down, staring into the eyes of the head. "Mimir?"

I frowned. The name seemed vaguely familiar.

"What?" the head grunted.

"You know who this is?" I asked.

Galin nodded, not taking his eyes off the head. "We're

interested in going to Mimisbrunnr. Can you tell us how to get there?"

"No," said the head.

"Oi!" interrupted Gondul, "Tell the handsome sorcerer where to go, or I'll let the girls play soccer with you again."

Mimir's features contorted into an expression of abject terror. "No, not that."

"Remember how Hildr made you listen to her talk for hours about her recurring dream of being a cat? And the one about mushrooms? No one else will listen to her."

"Please no! It just kept going. I can't get away. I have no legs."

"Then tell the sorcerer what he wants to know," said Gondul through clenched teeth.

Mimir's eyes flicked back to Galin. He began to speak quickly. "You can find Mimisbrunnr in the roots of Yggdrasill—"

"We've looked there," I cut in.

"Did you bring Gjallarhorn?" he asked quickly.

I was thoroughly confused at this point. Mimir, Gjallarhorn?

"No," said Galin.

"Well, you need to blow the horn to reveal the well," Mimir shouted.

Galin leaned over and fixed Mimir with his dark gaze. "Where can we find Gjallarhorn?"

Mimir's eyes flicked to Gondul, but he didn't answer.

Galin whirled. "You know where it is? You vowed to help us find Mimisbrunnr."

Gondul sighed, obviously annoyed. "One moment."

Without another word, she disappeared from the room.

Galin, the head, and I were left alone.

I stared at the head, finding myself moving closer. At last my curiosity was too much. "Your name is Mimir?"

The head blinked.

"I recognize the name," I continued, "but I can't remember where—"

"I worked for Odin," Mimir grumbled.

I didn't understand why he was so tetchy. We'd just released him from a suitcase. I'd have thought it would have been pretty unpleasant to be kept in a box for who knew how many years.

"As a head?" I asked. "What did you do for him?"

"I was decapitated by my enemies, but Odin revived me."

"And Mimisbrunnr is named after you?"

"Yes," croaked the head. "I was the pool's guardian when I had a body."

I nodded. *Oh, this makes a lot more sense now.*

Mimir's eyes narrowed. "Why do you wish to visit the well?"

"To drink from it," Galin said.

Mimir's eyes widened. "You know that such knowledge comes at a cost. Odin lost his eye, I lost my entire body."

I did *not* know that.

Galin shook his head. "I have no other choice. I am willing to accept whatever penalty I must pay—"

At that moment, the door to Odin's apartment burst open, and Gondul returned with Hildr in tow. Hildr rushed into the room, her face flushed with excitement. "Mimi! My dearest friend."

"Don't leave me alone with her!" shouted Mimir frantically.

"You're such a good listener, Mimi."

"I have somewhere else to be right now—" continued Mimir.

"I had a dream about a herd of cows," she began. "But then they were not cows at the same time. They were cows, but not cows—"

"Hildr," Gondul barked, pointing at Galin. "You need to give this man your drinking horn."

"It's *my* horn."

Gondul's schoolmarm voice returned. "Give him the horn, or I'll put Mimir away."

With an exaggerated sigh, Hildr passed her horn to Galin. Then she snatched Mimir from the bed, and ran with him from the room.

CHAPTER 26

GALIN

For the second time in as many days, we flew above the roots of Yggdrasill. I tried to concentrate on flying, and not on the feel of Ali's legs pressed against mine, or her arms wrapped around my waist. Or how she'd looked in that red underwear …

I had to concentrate on the flying.

After Hildr left, I'd managed to call a portal, and we travelled to the Citadel in Midgard. From there, we took a moth, and soared back into the Well of Wyrd.

I had Gjallarhorn at my hip, but I didn't reach for it yet. As we flew, I scribed *sowilo*, directing the glowing spell to fly along with us.

We soared over roots that twined together, glistening in the dark.

"Galin," whispered Ali, "are you ready?"

I nodded, finally reaching for Gjallarhorn. It was a ram's horn rimmed with gold. Runes I didn't recognize were carved into the sides. If I had more time I would have studied it, learned its secrets. I could sense ancient gods' magic within it—also a great deal of stale mead.

What had Hildr been thinking, using this relic as a beer cup? Criminal.

I shook out the last drops, then used my thumb to pop a cork out of the mouthpiece. Drawing in a breath, I blew, the air buzzing between my lips. The sound started small, like a bugle or a trumpet. Then it grew, louder and louder. I ran out of breath, but the horn kept sounding.

Ali withdrew one of her arms from around my waist, and pointed to the roots below. They'd begun to twist and move like a nest of serpents, intertwining and coiling upon themselves. Holding the sounding horn with one hand, I used my other to guide the moth lower. We swooped just above the writhing roots.

"There," Ali shouted over the noise of the horn.

In the dim light my eyesight was not as sharp as hers, but I could just make out the mouth of a cave.

Pulling its antennae, I directed the moth downward and into the opening. Powerful magic washed over me as we crossed inside, a deep thrumming that seemed to hum in my heart and bones.

"What is that?" whispered Ali.

"Magic." I guided us into the cave—an enormous cavern of wood, easy to navigate—the walls glowing with faint silver light.

As we descended, dark magic swirled around us, until I could no longer see where we were going. "I need to set it down. We can walk from here." Through the haze, I guided the moth down to the roots.

I dismounted, and Ali slipped off after me. I swayed for a moment before I got my bearings, like a sailor stepping from a ship to dry land.

"Galin," Ali said, "what about what Mimir said? That there are consequences to drinking the water?"

"I don't think we have a choice, Ali. We don't know how

else to defeat the draugr. Better to lose an eye or a hand than to lose all nine realms."

She shot me a nervous look. "But I wish it didn't have to be you."

"This is my responsibility to fix."

"I don't like it," she said quietly.

"Do you have a better idea?"

She shook her head. "I wish I did."

Around us the walls of the cave began to narrow. Small mushrooms, glowing faintly in the gloom, now dotted the root bark. They gave off a warm light.

"Foxfire," said Ali, studying the fungi. "Very rare. I saw them only once or twice in the Shadow Caverns."

We followed the mushrooms round the great coils of Yggdrasill's roots. A narrow path carved between them. As we made our way deeper, the cave began to fill with the sound of dripping water, echoing off the walls.

Ali's hand brushed against my arm. "We must be getting close."

I nodded. We rounded a gnarled root, and I saw that the cave ended with a strange formation of wood in the ground —a perfectly circular hole not far from us, about thirty feet wide. Roots ringed the edges and climbed down the walls.

My breath caught. *Mimisbrunnr.*

What I had initially thought was empty was actually filled with water. It was just that the liquid was so perfectly still and clear that it looked black. I only realized it was there when a drop of water from the cave's ceiling sent ripples racing across its surface.

"Do you see it?" whispered Ali.

I nodded. As we neared the well, I studied the roots at the edge of the water. The magic thrummed so strongly I could *hear* it.

Was the well the source of Yggdrasill's magic, or was

Yggdrasill the source of the well's magic? Or did they feed each other?

I stood at the edge with an overwhelming mix of relief and foreboding. On the one hand, I was ready to learn how to escape Hel and defeat the draugr. On the other, I knew it was going to require a terrible sacrifice. Yet I would do anything to protect the nine realms.

I looked into the depths, half expecting to see the answers reflected there, but the crystal-clear water only revealed Yggdrasill's roots under the surface.

"Galin, look." Ali pointed to a large granite boulder, one of the few right at the water's edge. "I think this is what you're supposed to drink from."

I followed her onto the boulder. It extended a few feet into the water, creating a small platform. One end of a silver rod had been hammered into the rock, while the other end curled into a sort of hook. A silver teacup hung from the hook.

My throat still burned from the dragon blood, so I wasn't speaking much. Instead, I knelt and took the cup in my hand, then dipped it into the pool. As the water brushed my knuckles, I sucked in a short breath. I'd never felt anything so cold.

Holding my breath, I lifted the cup. Mimisbrunnr's water shimmered within it. It was strange to think this cup contained all the answers. How to defeat the draugr. How to free Hela so she would open the gates to Hel, willingly. Perhaps a new fate.

Ali's hand shot out, and she touched my arm, a fierce expression in her silver eyes. "I don't think you should do this."

"So you care for me then? Even without the mating bond."

"Yes. And I don't want your legs to fall off or something."

"Neither do I." And yet, it was my job to fix this.

Dread shivered up my spine when I looked into the cup

again. I realized, with a shock, that I was still holding out a glimmer of hope for Ali. And I didn't want to lose that chance with her by turning into a severed head like Mimir.

But I'd come this far to stop the draugr, and warriors like me didn't have the luxury of finding a more comfortable plan.

"Wait." As she reached for my arm again, I lifted the cup and drank. The water touched my lips, sliding down my throat, glacial.

I tried to inhale, but my lungs had completely frozen. Again, I tried to inhale. Nothing.

I gripped my throat, even as a chill spread from my stomach. Out my arms, down my legs. My vision wavered. Distantly, I heard Ali calling my name.

My mind swarmed with shadows, suffocating darkness. Disorienting.

Then—I began to see things.

A glimmer in the depths. Slowly brightening, reddening, hot red blood washed over me. Cries of dying warriors rose up around me, the harsh voice of a raven squawking, the screaming of children, the iron clang of swords, the crowing of a rooster, growing louder, louder, changing, morphing into a deep bestial howling.

Fear gripped my heart. I'd seen this before, heard these sounds. A thousand years ago when the gods died, when the world was plunged into despair, when Ragnarok froze the earth. When I lost my soul, was cursed and imprisoned, when all hope was lost. When meaning was buried under an icy earth.

And I didn't find a glimmer of hope again until I met Ali, a bright spark in the darkness, our souls twined together. For a time.

My heart slammed in my chest as a creature moved in the darkness. I was spun around. The terrible howling filled the void. A massive jaw slammed shut around me, trapping me in its teeth, and just as I was swallowed, I realized it was Fenrir. The great wolf who heralded the beginning of Ragnarok.

In the great beast's stomach, ice-cold water filled me entirely. I couldn't move. I only sank, deeper and deeper. This was the end, I realized. No mortal should drink the water of Mimisbrunnr. I had paid the price for knowledge, and it was with my life. And all I wanted was to tell Ali that I still loved her.

Then a strong hand pulled me from the water. I gasped, finally drawing in breath. Rejoicing as my lungs filled with warm air.

I gasped, coughing out the last of Mimisbrunnr's water onto the rock. Then, I straightened.

"Galin?" said a deep voice.

I twisted round, confused. Instead of Ali, a large man stood over me. He wore silver chainmail, and a gleaming sword hung at his hip. A thick hood hid his face, except one bright blue eye, like a sapphire caught in a sunbeam.

"Odin," I rasped. "But you're dead.

"So I am." The King of the Gods' voice resonated through my entire body like powerful magic. "But part of my soul remains in these waters."

He took a step closer. "You have something you wish to know."

"Yes."

"Do you accept the price?"

Ice spread through my chest. I was going to learn what I needed to know, but I would pay for it dearly.

"I accept the price."

"What is it you wish to know?"

"Hela has closed the gates to Hel. The dead are ravaging the lands of the living. There's a draugr horde threatening

Vanaheim and Midgard. Hela refuses to stop this. How do I stop them?"

Odin's blue eye blinked slowly. "To defeat the draugr, you need Surtr's sword."

This was not what I wanted to hear. "Surtr the fire giant? King of Muspelheim?"

He inclined his head. "Yes. I will tell you how to defeat him."

Odin drew a small piece of parchment from under his chainmail and showed it to me. I sucked in a short breath as I looked at the runes scrawled on the page—a new spell, one I'd never seen before.

"I see," I whispered, reading them. "That would work."

"Once you have the sword you can use it to destroy the draugr."

He began to turn away from me.

"Wait," I said quickly. "This will only happen again unless Hela gets what she wants. She wants to be free of Hel. How can she break down the walls?"

"Surtr's sword is the only thing that can pierce the iron walls that surround Hel. Carve a hole in the wall. But know if you do that, the souls of the dead will overwhelm the lands of the living. All the mortals will perish."

"So there is no way to save them?"

Odin's sapphire eye swept down to the runes on my chest. "Tell Hela you failed. Remain in Hel. Live for eternity as the consort of a goddess? You'll have power, immeasurable magic."

I shook my head. "Are you certain there is no other way?"

Odin paused, running a hand through his beard.

"There is, but it is difficult. If you fail, all will be lost."

Hope thrilled within me. "Tell me."

"Reverse Ragnarok. Bring back the gods."

I stared at him. This *was* tempting. I wanted the gods alive again, to reverse Ragnarok. The world thriving with spring, with life—with the magic of the gods. And yet … it hadn't gone well when I raised Hela. This could have unforeseen consequences.

"You have already raised a goddess," Odin went on. "You must do the same for the rest of us. You've seen where our bones lie in Asgard. Cast that spell there, and we will rise again. This is the only way."

And with that, he began to fade, slipping into the shadows until only his blue eye remained. Then he was gone.

"Galin." Ali's voice sounded distant. "Galin?"

I cracked open my eyes. I was freezing cold, lying on the granite boulder, Mimisbrunnr's icy water only inches away. Ali crouched next to me, one of her hands pressed on my bare chest.

"Are you all right?" She scanned me from top to bottom. "It doesn't look like you lost anything."

I nodded weakly. Now that the vision had faded, exhaustion remained, and I felt chilled to the bone.

Ali's beautiful silver eyes filled with hope. "And you know about the draugr? You know how to get rid of them."

I nodded again. Relief spread over her face, and without saying a word she hugged me. "Thank you Galin."

I breathed in her scent, enjoying the feel of her warmth next to me.

When she pulled away, I sat up. "Ali, it's not going to be easy."

Except when I tried to speak, no sound came out of my mouth. I tried again. "It's not going to be easy."

Silence—just the rushing of breath from my mouth.

Fear clawed at my heart. Something was wrong. I could not make a sound.

Ali stared at me. "Galin, are you all right?"

My heart was a wild beast. If I couldn't speak, I couldn't

use magic. I tried to just say Ali's name. A bitter taste filled my mouth. Grimacing, I spat, expecting blood, but instead a fine black dust escaped my lips.

She touched the side of my face. "You can't speak?"

I nodded, then dipped my finger in Mimisbrunnr's icy water. I traced on the granite a pair of words: "Price paid."

Disappointment crushed my chest, but I couldn't say I was surprised. Odin had lost an eye, Mimir had lost his body. It made sense that I was to lose the thing that defined my existence.

By taking my voice, Mimisbrunnr had also stolen my magic.

CHAPTER 27

ALI

I stared, watching as Galin pulled off pieces of Yggdrasill's bark, not understanding what he was doing. He spent a few minutes crushing up the foxfire fungus into a sort of pulp, then filled Hildr's horn with the glowing juice.

He could not tell me what he was doing, nor ask for help.

For just a moment, his expression looked anguished. Then, he seemed to school his features again—perfectly stoic.

As we walked back toward the moth, I stole a glance at him. His eyes were fixed on the path, his expression stony.

He must have been devastated. Unlike when he'd been a lich, I was certain this change was permanent. Odin, the King of the Gods, had sacrificed an eye to the well. If it were possible to get it back, he'd have done it.

I'd always viewed it as my job to free the Night Elves from the Shadow Caverns. Just like Mom had said—I was supposed to be the North Star. And I'd done it. With Galin's help, I'd brought them out into the light again. But if someone had taken from me the one thing I viewed as my purpose, I would have been gutted.

But I couldn't read a thing in Galin's face.

When we finally reached the moth, he turned to me. He probably thought his expression was stoic, but I could see the exhaustion in his eyes.

Galin knelt next to the moth and began to untie it. I expected him to climb on, but as soon as he freed the beast, he released it. The moth soared up toward the light, and I stared, baffled.

"Galin, did you learn how to defeat the draugr? What are we doing?"

He held up one of the pieces of pale bark, and dipped his finger into the fungus juice. At last, I understood what that was for as he began to write. *We need Surtr's sword. From Muspelheim.*

I frowned at it. Surtr. The name rang a bell—a figure from some of my childhood stories. "He's a giant, right? A ... fire giant?" And Muspelheim was the realm of fire—a place I'd absolutely never wanted to visit.

Galin nodded.

"We're supposed to steal from a fire giant. In the realm of fire."

Galin wrote, *We use a spell.*

I felt very confused at this point. "You know a spell? But how are you going to do magic without being able to speak?"

He pointed at me with a purple-stained finger.

"I don't have the wand."

He arched a quizzical eyebrow, and I understood the meaning.

"Right, I've done it before. But I'm not sure I can replicate it."

He gestured at me to try. Then, he wrote, *To Vanaheim.*

I straightened. I still didn't quite see how this was going to work, but I was willing to give it a shot. Galin slipped behind me and gently took hold of my wrists. Slowly we began to scribe the runes of the portal spell.

He might be missing his voice and his magic, but he was still warm. I inhaled his smoke and sage scent, leaning against him. It wasn't exactly an embrace, but I liked the feel of his body against mine, his perfectly etched muscles.

I still wanted him to admit he wanted me, that he'd been lying. But how to do that if he didn't have a voice?

Focus, Ali.

As my finger carved through the air, I felt the magic of Yggdrasill resonate within me. I tried to think of love, of family. But my mind refused to stay put. Instead I kept thinking about Galin, worrying about his missing voice, and that brief flicker of anguish in his dark eyes. And yes, maybe I was thinking about the feel of his powerful arms against mine, the movement of his thickly corded muscles…

Once I'd slashed my finger down, executing the final rune, I twisted round to face him, to tell him I hadn't been focused. But as I did, the air in front of me began to shimmer. With a loud pop, a portal opened.

He smiled, victorious, and the electric crackle of magic hummed over us.

Just a moment later, we reappeared in my quarters in Vanaheim. Here, the sun was setting, casting rosy light and long shadows over the room.

I was relieved to see that the temple soldiers and workmen had been industrious in our absence. All the burned furniture had been removed, the floor cleaned. The troll's head was completely absent. The windows were open, presumably to clear out the smoke smell, giving a view of the clear pool outside.

I knew I should go straight to Swegde and the council, but I was starving and exhausted. And even though the servants had no way of knowing I'd be back, the usual arrangement of fruit, bread, cheese, and cured meats had been laid out for me—just in case.

I popped a handful of grapes into my mouth, then a large hunk of bread. Across from me, Galin gave me a funny look.

"Are you hungry?" I gave him a devilish smile. "I mean assuming you feel things?"

With a wry smile, he picked up an apple and bit into it.

With my muscles burning, I looked around for somewhere to sit. The singed sofa was gone, and the chairs. Grabbing another hunk of bread and cheese, I crossed to my bedroom, breathing an inward sigh of relief when I saw that my bed was still there—unburned, freshly made. A rosy gold duvet that looked divine.

"I'm going to lie down," I called out, and collapsed on top of the bed.

Galin leaned against the doorframe, arms folded. Shadowy magic drifted off his bare chest, midnight eyes fixed on me.

I scooted over, patting the bedspread next to me. "You can lie down too if you like."

Gripping my bread and cheese, I rolled over, and I felt the bed shift as Galin lay down next to me.

In moments I was fast asleep.

* * *

I DIDN'T KNOW how long I'd slept—only that I woke to the sound of an embarrassed yelp. Opening my eyes, I saw a Vanir guard standing at the door to my bedroom. Moonlight filtered into the room.

"Oh, I'm so sorry miss—Empress. I didn't realize you and the"—he swallowed—"King of Hel had returned. Together."

I blinked, realizing that I'd fallen asleep on the cheese, and it was now mashed to my face.

"Can you tell Swegde that I'm back?" I whispered, not wanting to wake Galin.

"Of course, your Majesty.

I looked to Galin. He lay on his back, his eyes closed. His bare chest moved slowly up and down. Asleep, he looked no less intimidating than awake, like a chiseled god. I was certain that if I tried to so much as touch him, he'd jerk awake, muscles tensing. My gaze swept down his body, the V of his abs—what the valkyries called his *sex lines.*

Pulling my gaze away, I stood quietly. While he slept, I changed into a clean set of leather clothes, then slipped out of the door and into the sitting room.

As I did, Swegde rushed in.

I lifted a finger to my lips.

"Is everything all right?" Swegde said breathlessly. "Why didn't you let me know you'd returned? Why are you standing like you've been injured?"

"I'm fine. We had a bit of a run-in with some giant wolves. But all that practice throwing knives turned out to be really useful after all."

He frowned. "Wolves?"

I held up my hands. "Everything is fine. I wasn't hurt."

Swegde didn't look very convinced. "What about Mimis-brunnr? Did you find it?"

"Yes."

His expression relaxed, then suddenly tightened again. "And where's Galin?"

Why did I feel defensive? "Do you always have this many questions? Galin is sleeping." I lowered my voice. "How are things here? What's up with the draugr horde?"

Swegde's face fell. "The monsters are at the gates. I've brought all our people into the city, but we only have enough food for a week."

My stomach clenched. Here I'd been napping on a wheel of cheese as my people prepared to starve.

"Show me the draugr," I said. "I'll fill you in on what happened on the way."

"Of course, Empress."

We hurried through the temple and then outside. As Swegde led me out towards the walls of the city, I told him how we'd climbed Yggdrasill, that a giant eagle had flown us to Asgard, how I'd seen the graves of the gods. I told him we'd narrowly avoided being eaten by wolves. When I got to the valkyries, Swegde's eyes widened.

"They tried to seduce Galin?"

"I wouldn't call it seduction. It was more like screaming that they wanted to shag him."

Swegde blew out a low whistle. "Wow."

"That was part of the reason I had to fight their leader."

"You fought a valkyrie?" Swegde went still.

"Yup, and I threw Skalei and hit her!"

Swegde clapped me on my back as we started walking again. "That's my girl." He was beaming, his eyes flashing with pride.

When we reached the ramparts, the stone walkways that swept over the outskirts of the city, dread started to steal my breath. A sea of the dead spread out before us.

The horror of seeing thousands of ravenous draugr in every direction overwhelmed me. We stood no chance against them—not without Surtr's sword.

"Swegde," I said. "We must get back to my quarters. I need to wake Galin. Then we need to figure out how to steal Surtr's sword."

CHAPTER 28

ALI

This time, I didn't hesitate to wake Galin.

"Galin," I shouted. "Galin, wake up."

"Mgggppht?" He groaned, then slowly opened his eyes.

I grabbed the notebook I kept by my bedside, in case he needed to speak. A pen lay wedged between the pages. "We need to go now, Galin. Like right now."

He scribbled, *Is everything okay? Are you hurt?*

"I'm fine. But the city isn't. It's surrounded by hundreds of thousands of draugr. I need to learn magic, right now, or we're fucked."

Galin's eyes widened, and he wrote frantically, *Are you certain of this?*

"Do you think I would have woken you if I weren't? I just got back from the wall. There is a sea of draugr, endless. Swegde says we have a week's worth of food at best, then all of Vanaheim starves." Guilt curled through me when I thought of how they'd been leaving food out for me. "Teach me magic. We have to fix this now."

He was still scribbling, but I wanted to get moving now. Without waiting for Galin to respond, I turned around and began to practice scribing the runes to the portal spell.

Galin sidled up behind me. I expected him to direct my hands, so I could focus solely on the incantation and emotional part of the magic, but instead he pulled my arms down to my sides.

"What are you doing? Now I have to start over." I pushed up with my hands, ready to begin the spell again, but again Galin held them at my sides.

"Galin!"

Galin turned me round so that I faced him, then he pointed to the bed.

"Sure, but not now, Galin." My cheeks reddened as I realized I didn't even know what he'd been asking.

He pointed to the bed again, and this time I saw that the notebook was spread open on it. "You want me to read that. Right." I picked it up.

We can fight the fire giant with ice. I spoke to a remnant of Odin's soul, and much knowledge was passed down to me. I learned how to kill the draugr, and I learned the runes of the spell for cold—or more specifically ice. This is what we'll use to defeat the fire giants and steal Surtr's sword. The emotion for the cold spell is fear.

Below the note, he'd drawn a series of runes.

"Fear!" I breathed. "That's perfect. I have that in spades right now." I inhaled a shaky breath at this sacred knowledge we'd been given by Odin himself. Then, I met Galin's gaze. "All right. Let's learn this spell."

I glanced at the runes. With Galin unable to speak, I wasn't sure how I was going to learn to pronounce any new ones. But as I read through them, I realized I recognized all of them. Slowly I read through the spell. Galin watched me, listening carefully. When I was done I looked to him. He nodded.

The next step was to practice the scribing. Galin slipped

behind me and took hold of my wrists. I didn't exactly need his help, but I let him guide my hands anyway.

Slowly we worked through the runes. Five, ten, twenty times. By the time we were going through the twenty-second or twenty third round, my stomach rumbled loudly.

I sighed and grabbed another chunk of bread from the table to gnaw on. "Give me a minute."

Galin pulled out the notebook.

Very good. You've got the words and the movements down. Now, you just need to channel your fear.

I smiled. "That won't be much of a problem. When we get to the fire giant, I will have plenty of fear."

Fear was easy. I had tons of experience with it. Shit, most of my time was spent trying to keep the damn emotion at bay. Right at this moment, I worried about my brother trapped in Hel. I worried about my people who would all be consumed by a massive horde of draugr if I fucked this up. I worried that the fire giant would burn us to death. I even worried about how Galin was going to handle the loss of his voice. This spell was going to be a piece of cake.

I straightened my back, and began to both scribe and incant the spell. To get my heart racing, I recalled the time I'd been on the fire escape, trapped by a crowd of draugr. Then I imagined what it would be like to be outside the castle walls at this very moment. Surrounded by draugr, a descending wave of death.

I slashed a rune as I imagined their desiccated bodies pressing in on me, tearing at my flesh. I scribed another as they scented my blood. A rune for hungry fingers. A rune for tearing flesh. I scribed the last rune as icy fear filled my heart, as I imagined the draugrs' cries as they began to eat me alive.

A chill raced down my arm. I closed my eyes, allowing

myself to be overcome with terror—the sense that I'd just lost everything I'd worked so hard for. The fear of dying alone. My heart filled with ice as draugr stole everything from me.

My lungs were full of arctic air, my skin subzero. *So cold, I am so cold.*

Then, a warm hand clamped over my mouth. A second hand gripped my wrist and pulled my scribing hand down, then drew me into a tight embrace, pulling my body against warm muscle.

Shivering, I leaned against Galin, allowing him to warm me. As his breath heated the skin of my neck, I moved with each rise and fall of his chest.

Slowly, the chill dissipated, my muscles thawing. I opened my eyes, and gasped. I'd encased the table of food with ice.

"I did it!" I shouted. "Oh my gods!"

I twisted round, and without thinking threw my arms around Galin. His body went rigid, and I wondered what he was thinking. But there wasn't much time to spend mulling that over.

"Let's head to Muspelheim."

CHAPTER 29

ALI

Two hours of riding were behind me, and I was fighting to stay awake. Sadly, since we'd never been to the realm of fire, a portal was not an option. We were traveling all the way on horseback, and time was of the essence.

After a quick message sent to the council, Swegde had shown us the route toward the fire realm. He led us out of the city through narrow underground tunnels that seemed to stretch on forever. At their exit, on the other side of the river, we mounted horses already packed with bags of gear; Swegde had sent word ahead.

Then we'd ridden all day through forests and fields, until we reached the desert. A canopy of stars spread over us, and dry earth beneath us.

In the moonlight, Galin sat on his horse, eyes straight ahead, looking perfectly at peace. I pulled a piece of bread from my bag, chewing on it with a bit of cheese, washing it down with water.

Normally, burglary requires running reconnaissance, establishing movements and patterns of the guards. We'd need a floor plan, a safe house. But according to Galin, Surtr would invite us in. I guessed I'd trust that he knew what he was talking about.

As the sun began to rise, I saw we were in a barren plain. I'd grown up underground, and the light here was blinding.

As I shielded my face with my hands, Galin handed me a hat. It shadowed my eyes, a blessing in this overpowering glare.

Hour after hour, we moved forward under the heat of the sun. Lizards skittered between scattered bushes. Above us vultures began to circle, and sweat poured down my temples. It was getting seriously hot, the ground cracked and dusty. Sand caught in my throat.

I was parched, but Galin seemed to have an uncanny knack for finding watering holes. Every hour or two, we'd stop to refill our canteens, drink deeply, and eat some of the dried fruit and nuts he'd brought with him.

But I hadn't slept properly in days now, and by dusk I was borderline delirious. As the sun set behind distant mountains, it stained the sky with shades of violet and crimson, wild colors I'd never seen in the sky. Until at last, it dipped beneath the horizon.

Blessed night swept over us.

As a Night Elf, I craved the dark, welcomed it like a long-lost lover.

When the moon started to rise, Galin reined in his horse, gesturing that I should get off mine. While he tended to the horses and set up camp, I started collecting firewood. There wasn't much, and most of it was covered in thorns, but I managed to find enough for a small fire.

In the meantime, Galin had constructed a fire pit, and set up a pair of small boulders to sit on next to it. I dropped down next to him, groaning as my tired legs rebelled.

He pulled out his notebook. *Ok?*

I nodded with a tired smile. "Just looking forward to getting rid of the draugr."

I half expected him to cast a spell to light the fire, but of course that wasn't an option anymore. So instead, he piled up some small twigs and lit them with a match. Then he stoked the fire, carefully adding small amounts of wood until he'd built a bed of coals.

As I watched the coals glow in the gathering darkness, Galin returned to his rucksack and retrieved an iron grate, a handful of small potatoes, and a bunch of green vegetables I didn't recognize. After a life underground, I was just learning to identify vegetables and fruit. He organized the ingredients on top of a flat rock, then began to cook.

First he sprinkled everything with salt and pepper, then he rested the grate between the stones. Carefully, he arranged the potatoes and vegetables on top, then drizzled them with oil.

As it all cooked, he sat back on his heels, using a small stick to turn the vegetables. A rich aroma filled the air, and my stomach rumbled in response.

It must have been loud enough for Galin to hear, because he looked at me and grinned. Then he turned back to the fire. He sprinkled more salt and pepper on everything. When it had thoroughly roasted, he plucked the potatoes and greens and arranged them on plates.

I devoured the potatoes with a ferocity I'd never known. I was absolutely famished, and they were perfect. I ate without speaking, alternating between the greens and potatoes. When I finally started to feel full, I looked up.

Galin was watching me, a bemused expression on his face. He flipped open his notebook. *Hungry?*

I wiped the back of my sleeve over my mouth. "It was the best food I've ever eaten."

I stood up and stretched my legs. Darkness surrounded

us, and the cool desert air was nearly still. An owl hooted in the distance, but otherwise it was quiet.

As I yawned, Galin unrolled a bedroll. I knew the draugr were at our gates, but if I didn't sleep, I was going to stop functioning soon.

I kicked off my boots and crawled onto the bedroll, then pulled a blanket out of my backpack. My legs still trembled with fatigue, but the ground was surprisingly soft. Next to me Galin lay on his own bedroll. The fire burned at our feet, and I found that I was surprisingly cozy.

Slowly the fire died, and the stars came out. They spread over us in a magnificent display of sparkling light. I identified Aurvandil's toe and Karlvagn.

I was going through them a second time, when I noticed something strange. Up in the mountains, close to the horizon, was a faint orange light. As I squinted at it, it grew brighter.

There—the realm of fire glowed in the distance like a little ember in the night.

"Galin," I whispered, "we found Muspelheim."

CHAPTER 30

ALI

*J*woke to the rising sun stroking the sky with orange. Galin was already awake, and the scratching of his pencil over the notebook was what had woken me up.

As I sat up, he handed me the notebook.

We should go. I don't want to be caught out here in the midday heat.

While I pulled on my boots, Galin strapped my bedroll to my horse. I was still half groggy with sleep, so it took me a minute to realize that he had already packed up our entire campsite. The fire was out, the plates and bowls put away. As I turned to thank him, he handed me my horse's reins.

With hats on, we set out across the desert, horses side by side, the sun warming our backs. Around us, birds flitted through the thorny brush. Little lizards basked on rocks, watching us carefully.

I hummed to myself, alternating between Beyoncé and Rick Roll. In front of us, hills rose off the desert floor, climbing rocky and barren until they became dark mountains at the edge of the horizon.

We followed little game trails up the steep slopes. We

rode for another hour, climbing higher and higher, as below us the desert spread out like a faded blanket, dusty and forlorn. When it became too much for the horses, we slipped off them and set off on foot.

As we climbed, a faint haze filled the air. With it came the acrid scents of smoke and sulfur. We hiked all day, passing through the foothills and into the lower slopes of the mountains.

Late in the afternoon, we were climbing up a steep slope when Galin suddenly stopped. Above us a dark shadow snaked along the ridgeline—too even to be natural.

As we approached, I could see a wall of stone. Not massively high like the iron wall that surrounded Hel. More like twenty feet of ragged rock, imposing with looming parapets. They could be hiding any number of men.

"What is that?" I asked.

He flipped open his notebook and gestured to where he'd previously written *Muspelheim*.

"Right. Okay." I didn't press him for more information. A sense of unease quieted me.

We'd followed along below the wall for about a mile when I saw the guard tower rising above us—a ruddy stone that gleamed in the sun. It had a clear view of the valley below.

I sensed that Galin planned to walk right up to it. My instinct was to scout the position and learn the movements of any guards.

"What's the plan, Galin? What did you mean when you said we would be invited in?"

He paused to pull out his notebook and write, then handed it to me. *I'm going to tell them I'm King of Hel, second in command to Hela. They'll agree to meet the companion of a goddess.*

"Oh, I see …" I said slowly. "And as the Empress of the

Vanir, I can tell them that I'm here to discuss an alliance with the elves."

Galin shook his head vigorously as he wrote quickly on his pad. *The giants are extremely patriarchal. Surtr rules a small court of males. The only women in his kingdom are servants and the members of his harem.*

Oh gods. "Are you serious?"

Yes, Galin wrote. *They'll never accept a woman as a leader. They'll kill you immediately if they find out who you are.*

"Great!"

I'm going to tell them I'm Hela's emissary. And you are my servant.

I stared at him. I couldn't say I was psyched about this plan, but I didn't see much other choice.

"Fine," I said. "Let's go see what the giants have to say."

Galin crossed to the tower door and banged on it hard with his fist. The sound reverberated in the still mountain air.

For a moment there was only silence. Then, a gravelly voice called from within, "Who goes there?"

"Should I say something?" I whispered.

Galin shook his head, then banged the door again.

Twenty seconds passed before the door slowly creaked open. A seven-foot-tall giant stood in the doorway, glaring down at us with small eyes under bushy red eyebrows. A red beard covered most of his face. He was dressed in buckskin pants, and a chainmail vest that seemed a little too small for his thick arms and barrel chest. An iron mace rested on his shoulder.

"Who are you?" he growled at Galin, entirely ignoring me.

Galin handed him a folded piece of paper.

The giant opened it, then slowly read it. "I see," he said at last. "An emissary of the Queen of the Dead. You wish to meet with King Surtr?"

Galin nodded.

The giant gestured for Galin to follow him, and we started forward. But as soon as I moved, the giant's mace dropped in front of me.

"No foreign women are allowed in Muspelheim."

"I'm the sorcerer's assistant."

"No women."

His beady eyes met mine. They were the strangest part of him; while the rest was proportionally large, from his feet to his beard, his eyes were far too small for his face. And yet I still recognized their hungry expression when they swept down my body.

Gross.

"Look," I said, locking eyes with the giant, "this was supposed to be a surprise, but the thing is I'm not really Galin's assistant." I drummed my fingertips together.

"Who are you?" he growled.

"You can't tell anyone," I said in a stage whisper. "But I'm actually a gift to King Surtr. I'm to join his harem." Night Elves must have been a rarity in the realm of fire, I imagined. I'd add something exotic to his collection.

Galin shot me a furious look, but it wasn't like he could say anything.

"You're a whore?" asked the giant, sounding confused.

I cleared my throat. "I am a *courtesan*. Very unique and expensive. Does the king have any Night Elves in his harem?"

Still the giant didn't look convinced. "You're not dressed like a courtesan."

He had a point here. My leather pants and jacket were caked with dust. I smiled, batting my eyelashes. "We've been traveling rough, but give me a bath, clean lingerie, and a spritz of *eau de toilette*, and I'll satisfy your king like no woman's done before. He won't need a harem once he has me."

Galin's dark eyes were blazing as he looked at me.

"Do you want King Surtr to learn that you turned me away?" I went on.

"All right," grumbled the giant. "Better come in, miss. Mountain lions roam these hills, size of ponies. Make a snack out of you. We'll see what King Surtr has to say about you."

I started forward, but again the giant blocked my path. He pressed an old burlap sack into my hands. "You are to wear this."

"How exactly am I supposed to do that?"

"Put it over your head. We can't have outsiders, courtesans or otherwise, learning the layout of Muspelheim."

I looked at the rough fabric of the sack. Once I put it over my head, I'd be practically defenseless. I'd just told a lecherous giant that I was a courtesan.

Still, what other choice did I have? I'd already fully committed. If I backed out now, I sensed he'd throw both Galin and me out. We had a sword to steal, and that was the important thing. I took a deep breath, then pulled the bag over my head.

As my eyes adjusted to the darkness, I heard the giant telling Galin he needed one as well.

While I stood, unable to see, a hand gripped mine. It took me a moment to realize it was Galin's.

"Thanks," I whispered.

The giant grunted, then the ground shook as he began to walk away from us. We followed the sound of his footfalls, passing through the interior of the tower, then back outside. I could tell because the light changed, and the mountain wind pushed the burlap against my face. Growing up in the caverns, I supposed I'd gotten used to functioning without a sense of sight.

Almost immediately, we started down a slope. The scent of smoke grew stronger, and mixed with a rank sulfur smell.

I kept expecting to stumble, but Galin's firm grip kept me upright. I thought the giant must have been leading him, because somehow he managed to make his way forward without falling.

We walked until the path flattened again, but it didn't get easier. Now, the air was thick with smoke, the smell of sulfur so pungent that my eyes watered. I reminded myself why we were here—without the sword, the world would end at the hands of the draugr.

So I could deal with some discomfort.

At last, the footfalls stopped. A door creaked, then the interior of the sack darkened as we were led inside.

"Stairwell!" the giant called out.

He didn't say if it was up or down, so I awkwardly pedaled my foot in the air till I realized we were heading down again.

The scents of smoke and sulfur disappeared, but the air kept growing hotter. Sweat wet my brow and began to trickle down my neck.

After what seemed like ages, the giant stopped, and a second door creaked open. Voices greeted us—the deep, gravelly tones of giants mixed with more feminine notes. In the background, music floated in the air. The voices went quiet as we crossed into this new room.

Galin gave my hand a squeeze, then let go.

"Who the Hel is this?" a deep voice boomed.

An awkward silence fell, then the burlap sack was unceremoniously ripped from my head. I gasped, both at the fresh air and at what I saw before me.

Galin stood next to me, free from the burlap as well. The giant guard stood beside him.

A new giant dwarfed us, at least ten feet tall. He had the same bright red hair as the guard. His black silk pajamas draped over a large stomach, and his pig-like eyes squinted at us. A gold crown marked him as the king.

By my side, Galin was frantically writing in his notebook.

So this was Surtr. Looked like a charmer. What I didn't see was a sword on him.

"I said," he growled, "who the Hel are you?"

Galin ripped a page from his notebook and handed it to the giant king.

"What in the dead gods' name is this?" said Surtr, holding the paper close to his face. He read slowly before speaking again. "I see. You're really Hela's king? King Galin?"

Galin nodded, gesturing to the shadowy runes tattooed on his chest.

"And you?" he said, turning to me.

I forced a smile that may have been a grimace. "I'm a gift. Hela is giving me to you as part of your harem—a gesture of goodwill from the goddess."

He looked me over then, his beady eyes roving unashamedly over my body. I wanted to puke. "A little small for my taste," he said at last. "But I've never had a Night Elf before." He drummed his fingertips together, then licked his lips. "Delectable. I'm sure we can find room for you in my harem."

I bowed deeply, even as bile rose in my throat. "Yes, my liege."

Think of the draugr. Think of the draugr. We are here for a reason.

CHAPTER 31

ALI

$\mathcal{I}$ followed behind a willowy elf with long white hair. She turned to frown at me. "Normally I'd take you straight to your room, but considering your state, I think we should go to the baths first."

What I wanted to know was where Surtr's sword was, but I had a feeling that if I came out and asked, I might find myself being burned to death in a furnace. So instead I asked, "What is your role here, Asha?"

Asha's expression said I should already know the answer to my question. "I'm the Madame of King Surtr's harem, along with my sister."

"You're the head of the harem?"

"Yes, and King Surtr's main consort," she said primly. "Now if you'll just follow me, I'll show you to the baths. The stench on you is not appealing."

"How did you end up here?" I asked. "You look like a High Elf."

"I ended up here after Ragnarok," she said with a sense of finality. "Here we are." She stopped at a door marked *Baths*. As she pushed it open, I was immediately enveloped by a cloud of steam.

I blinked in the hot vapor, then crossed inside.

Asha gestured at a stony pool of steaming water, inset into ivory marble. "There you are. The king does not like his women filthy." She huffed. "At least not in the way that you are currently filthy."

I smiled. There was absolutely no way King Surtr was getting filthy with me, but I played along, hoping to find out more about the sword.

In any case, the bath looked amazing, with steam rising from a large, clear pool. I pulled my shirt over my head. When I could see again, Asha was staring at me. I wasn't ashamed of my body, but there was something about her expression that made me instinctively self-conscious. Her gaze seemed … professionally critical.

"Is everything okay?" I asked sharply.

"Your breasts are the size of oranges. He likes them larger." She tsked, then suddenly shouted, "Shauna! I need your help."

An instant later another woman appeared in the doorway, her appearance identical.

"What do you think?" said Asha to her twin.

Shauna looked me over, shaking her head. "They're pert. Not proportional to her hips. Her ass is nice and round, which will be good for the twerking."

"The *what?*"

"You know how to twerk, right?" they said in unison. "The dance."

Asha added, "Any courtesan should know."

I did not. And yet—could twerking get me close enough to Surtr to steal his sword? The seed of an idea started to bud in my mind.

Perhaps this *twerking* could save the world.

"I need to brush up on my twerking. But before I do that,

I'm going to bathe now," I said quickly. "Can I get a bit of privacy?"

Asha burst out laughing. "Privacy? Honey, this is a harem. There's no privacy here."

"Fine."

Fuck it. I pulled off my pants and slipped into the bath, wearing my bra and panties. The water was a little hot, but it felt amazing on my tired muscles. Closing my eyes, I submerged my entire body.

After a few seconds I popped my head out. Immediately I heard Asha's voice. "Well? What's your plan?"

"Plan?" I frowned. "What do you mean?"

She tossed her white hair behind her shoulders. "You're the first girl to be added to the king's harem in nearly one hundred years. He's going to want you to perform for him as soon as possible. To dance, play a musical instrument, sing—"

"I can sing," I offered.

"Oh, Surtr will like that. He loves a good tune. What songs do you know?"

"Well, my favorite song is called 'Rick Roll.'" I began to hum a little bit of the melody. Then I added, "He was a great warrior."

"Honey," said Asha. "That song is *not* sexy. You need to sing something seductive. You're supposed to be putting King Surtr in the mood."

I smothered my irritation. "Rick Roll" was seductive. Taking a deep breath, I launched into one of my other classical favorites—"Baby Shark."

The sisters clamped their hands over their ears, looking furious.

"No!" said both harem sisters simultaneously.

"That will definitely not work," Asha shouted. "In fact,

never sing that song again. I'm tempted to have you executed for that."

"Wait," I said frantically, "I was just warming up. How about this song?"

This time I began to sing the only Beyoncé song I knew: "Single Ladies."

This time Asha and Shauna didn't interrupt. In fact, when I stopped after finishing the first verse, the twins simply stared at me. I thought it was over. Then both their faces split into huge smiles.

"I want to hear more of that."

"She's Beyoncé," I said. "Once a great queen in Midgard. In fact, I had an iPod with her music on it. Sacred music."

"Oh my gods, can we listen to it?" The twins nearly shouted as they stood over me in the bath. They were both shaking with excitement.

I shook my head. "Unfortunately, I lost the iPod." The twins' faces fell. "But, I remember more songs—"

Shauna cut me off. "Will you teach us?"

This, I realized, was an opportunity. "Will you show me how to twerk?"

The twins exchanged a glance. "Yes."

"All right, this song is called 'Single Ladies' …"

As I luxuriated in the tub, I taught the twins the lyrics to "Single Ladies." They began to sing to one another, and I lay back in the hot water.

My mind drifted to all the things I had to do. I needed to learn to twerk, get close to the king. I needed to steal his sword.

And then once I'd stolen it, I needed to figure out how to call a portal. And that required love.

I thought back to the time on the cliff face, when the troll had been about to kill Galin. I tried to remember what emotions I'd been feeling then. Terror, fear, and panic, certainly. But to call the portal I was supposed to feel love, and I hadn't been feeling love at all. It made no sense.

"Ali?" said Asha suddenly.

I opened my eyes. "Yes?"

"Are you finished in the bath?"

It was—perhaps—time to get the sword. "I'm done."

"Good," she said, sounding relieved. "One of the guards stopped by. Surtr is asking for you."

"Did he say what he wanted?"

"He wants you in his quarters in ten minutes." Asha exchanged a look with Shauna. "He likes to try out new girls right away."

Gross. "Sounds fantastic." I stood. I was still wearing my underwear, and they were soaked. "Can you pass me a towel?"

Asha placed a towel on the edge of the bath. "I've left dry clothes for you on the bench. If you hurry, there should be enough time to teach you how to twerk."

She and Shauna left, and I climbed from the tub, warm water dripping down my body. I peeled off my soaking-wet underwear and wrapped the towel around me. As I dried off, I turned to look at the outfit the twins had left me—not so much an outfit as a tiny pile of lingerie. A pair of panties, a camisole that looked much too small. That was it.

The door creaked open. "Everything okay?" Asha asked.

"I'll be right out!"

I picked up the panties. The lace might have been black, but they were nearly transparent.

"Are you sure this is everything?" I called out.

"Yes," she called back.

Somehow I managed to squeeze myself into the panties and camisole. My boobs might have been only the size of oranges, but right now, they threatened to burst out. The chiffon barely extended as far as my belly button. Good thing

I could call Skalei at any time, because in this outfit there was nowhere I could have hidden a dagger.

"Hurry along please," Asha snapped.

I pushed open the door into the marble hall. Asha and Shauna were standing nearly directly in front of me. Shauna was drinking a large glass of white wine, while Asha held a pair of black stilettos. She pressed them into my hands. "Put these on."

As I stepped into the heels, the pair of elves looked me over for what felt like the thousandth time.

"She's cuter than I thought," said Asha at last. "In this outfit."

"Those panties really help extend her legs." Shauna took a sip of her wine.

Another forced smile. "Are you going to teach me this twerking thing or not?" *Because I need to steal from your king STAT.*

"All right, I'll show you," said Asha. She widened her legs and bent over, pointing her bum at me. She rested her hands on her knees, then started moving her hips, her butt bouncing like a ball. I found the movement transfixing.

I couldn't believe what I was seeing. Now *this* was a skill. "That's twerking? It is amazing."

Shauna rolled her eyes. "She's not even that good."

Asha spun round to face her sister, her eyes flashing angrily. "King Surtr *loves* it when I twerk for him. And now, that is what you must do."

I swallowed hard. When I twerked, I would not be as skilled as Asha. I'd just be waving my butt in the air.

Yes, I was helping to save the world. But this had to be the least dignified way to do it.

ALI

Five minutes later, I was following a giant guard up a long staircase of gleaming stones. I held the stiletto heels in one hand, and padded along behind him. The stone felt cool beneath my feet. The twins flanked me, like I might make a run for it or something.

At the top of the stairs, the guard stopped and knocked on an ornate set of iron doors decorated with metallic suns.

"Who is it?" Surtr said from the other side.

"I'm here with Asha, Shauna, and—" The guard looked down. "What's your name, girl?"

"Ali—Alina," I lied. I doubted that Surtr had heard of Ali the Empress of the Vanir, but I didn't want to risk it.

"And Alina, the Night Elf."

"Oh, come in, come in," boomed the king's voice.

The guard pushed the door open, and I got my first look at Surtr's chambers, sumptuously decorated. The king reclined on a large sofa at the far end, surrounded by servants. And to my relief, Galin sat in a chair nearby, looking intensely uncomfortable.

A thick red carpet covered the floor; everywhere there were cushions embroidered with gold and silver. Tables were piled with dates and grapes, cheese and spiced nuts. The thick scent of incense filled the air. In one corner, an elegant elf dressed in golden robes played a gentle acoustic guitar.

I didn't see a single sign of a sword.

"Alina, Alina." Surtr leered at me from across the room. "Come closer, little Night Elf." His feet rested on a massive ottoman. In one hand, he casually held a glass of wine the size of a bucket.

To his right, Galin had gone completely tense, shadows whipping from his body. His glare cut right through me, and although he held a glass of wine, he looked like he was on the verge of crushing it with his fist. Just as when he'd been in Hel, the whites of his eyes had turned entirely black.

Apparently, he did not approve of this plan.

"Ah, now I understand why Hela sent you," drawled the king. "This outfit is considerably more suitable." He frowned, then asked, "What are you wearing on your feet?"

I looked down at my bare toes. I'd forgotten to put on the stilettos.

"Nothing?" I said with a shrug.

Surtr grunted. "Put on the heels. And show me what you have prepared."

What would the valkyries do in this situation? Some battles involved swords. Others involved high heels. So I dropped them on the floor, and slipped into the ridiculous shoes.

I drew in a deep breath, opened my voice to sing "Single Ladies," then hesitated. If I continued to go along with Surtr's requests, eventually he was going to ask me for something I wouldn't offer him. The last time I'd been in this situation, I'd driven Skalei into an Emperor's heart.

And then what? I was surrounded by giants. Galin had no powerful magic without his voice.

Maybe now was the best time to ask about the sword.

"Well girl, are you going to sing or not?" said Surtr.

I cleared my throat. "Actually, I was thinking I might dance for you first."

"Oh really?" He grinned and flicked his bushy eyebrows up and down.

"The dance of my people, the Night Elves. A sword dance."

Surtr frowned, not moving.

"It is a seductive custom in the Shadow Caverns." I bit my lip. "And I was hoping to play with … your sword. I've heard yours is very large."

"Get the girl my sword!" bellowed the king. "Let her get a good grip on it."

I kept glancing at Galin, hoping we were on the same page. But it was hard to read anything in his shadowy gaze.

A guard ran from the room. A minute later he returned holding a massive weapon. I'd expected Surtr's blade to be large, but the giant's sword was nearly five feet long, the blade inscribed with glowing runes. At least it wasn't on fire.

"Hurry man!" The king rubbed his hands. "Give the girl my blade so I can see her dance."

I took the sword by the hilt, realizing the blade was actually quite hot. If I let it touch me I'd be burned. But I wasn't worried. While daggers were certainly my specialty, I'd spent plenty of time practicing with swords.

I tossed the blade into the air like a majorette's baton. I caught it one-handed, the blade pointing up. I locked my eyes on King Surtr, who leaned forward on the sofa—eager to see this exotic sword dance. I sashayed closer, smiling seductively.

I glanced again at Galin, hoping he understood what needed to happen next. But I could read nothing in his expression. He was staring at me, clutching his wine glass, his eyes clouded with black magic. *Give me a sign, Galin.*

But this was my chance, and I wasn't going to get another.

I pointed the sword at the giant king's chest.

King Surtr frowned, still unaware I was about to steal his sword. "This is part of your dance?"

"Galin!" I shouted. "Now."

Galin moved, but he was slow, stumbling out of his chair. The wine glass glinted in his hand, and I finally put it together. He was drunk.

Was he *kidding* me? I needed him by my side, channeling magic with me. Otherwise, the spell could hit him, too.

"What is this?" the king bellowed.

Time's up. I gripped the sword with one hand and began to chant the runes to the ice spell. The king's eyes widened, but I'd already launched into it, hoping Galin would be touching me by the time I finished.

"Stop her!" Surtr shouted.

It was too late for the king. I slashed the final rune and channeled all my terror into the spell. Instantly a blast of ice and snow flew out of me. It slammed into the fire giants, freezing them all.

The post-spell fatigue hit me, and it was my turn to stumble. I looked around.

Just as I'd feared, Galin had been hit with the ice spell, too.

Fuck. This was not part of the plan.

But since I was holding a smoldering hot sword, maybe I had a way to fix this. I rushed over to Galin and pressed the flat edge of the blade against the ice that encased him. Almost instantly, it began to melt. Within minutes, I'd freed him. He stared at me, eyes black as voids. He was still holding the freaking wine glass like his life depended on it.

"Are you ready?" I asked, panic rising in me.

Every muscle in his body had gone rigid, and Hela's

magic poured off him in swirls of black. He wasn't just drunk. He was filled with Hela's magic.

He cocked his head and stared at me, then shook his head. *No.*

"We need to go, Galin. What is going on with you?"

Galin shook his head again.

I spun away from him, then began casting the portal spell. I was halfway through it when I felt one of Galin's hands on my hip.

"Galin! I'm trying to focus on feeling love, and all I feel right now is deep fucking irritation mixed with fear. If you're not going to help, then don't interrupt."

I smelled something on him, something sickly sweet and familiar—fairy wine. I glanced at his glass of wine, half of it frozen.

That was what he'd been drinking—the same stuff that had made Barthol lose his mind, the fairy wine that inspired lust and madness.

A noise like a glass shattering refocused my attention. I spun just in time to see one of King Surtr's arms break free of the ice.

More ice magic? I had plenty of fear. But if I kept using that spell, I'd tire myself out fast. Another crack of breaking ice, and Surtr was nearly free.

Love—fairy wine could inspire love, and lust. I snatched the glass from Galin and slugged it back. It tasted better than it smelled, and already a delicious feeling spread through my body, giddy and bubbly. I had to fight the urge to laugh.

Across from me, Surtr ripped the ice off his head. He glared at me. Maybe he wasn't so bad …

Get it the Hel together, Ali.

The fairy wine was coursing through my veins now, and I felt beaming with love. I loved Galin, and Barthol, and the people in Vanaheim who were at risk. And more than anything I wanted to protect them.

I thought of Galin, and the look of hurt in his eyes when he learned he'd lost his voice for good. The way he kept looking after me.

I glanced at him, at the shockingly beautiful planes of his face. I had to get him to safety.

Gripping the sword in one hand, I slashed through the runes of the portal spell with the other. As I scribed the final one, I let all the bubbly love flow from me into the spell. With a scintillating flash, a portal cracked open.

I heard Surtr bellow, "Kill her!"

But I was already leaping through the portal, the sword tight in my hand.

CHAPTER 33

ALI

I fell into my quarters in Vanaheim, landing on my bed. The heated blade nearly seared my skin as I fell on top of it, but I rolled off quickly—just in time to see Galin jumping through the portal. It closed up behind him.

I shoved the hot sword onto the floor, then lay back on the silky blanket. The silk was pure ecstasy against my skin, and my pulse started racing.

I crawled to my knees, looking around. It was the middle of the night, and only the smoldering runes of Surtr's sword lit the room.

Where is Galin?

He stood at the foot of the bed, his eyes locked on mine. A savage thrill ran through me, hot and feral. My pulse started racing. The fairy wine clouded my mind, and I couldn't remember what we were supposed to be doing now.

The sword … the sword was important. I was supposed to do something with the sword.

But I couldn't focus with the fiery need that was building in me.

The night breeze rushing through the window kissed my

skin. I felt my nipples go hard against the delicate lace camisole.

Galin seemed to notice, and I bit my lip. I wanted him to tell me that he did desire me, but there was some reason he couldn't. Another cool breeze rippled over me, and blazing desire swept through me.

All I could think about was his smoky, masculine smell. I closed the distance between us. When I was within inches of him, he grabbed me by the waist and picked me up. Now, he was pressing me against the wall, hands pinning my hips against the cool stone. The feel of his fingers on my body seared my skin with hot lust. He slid his knee between my thighs, spreading my legs, dominating me.

I reached up and touched his cheek. "You are awfully close for a man who feels no desire." That was it—the thing I was supposed to be doing. I was supposed to be getting him to admit that even without the mating bond, he wanted me. He'd said he felt nothing for me, that he was dead inside. That all his desire had been extinguished. And now, a wicked part of me wanted to make him regret ever saying that.

There was the sword … I glanced at the sword on the floor, trying to remember why it was important.

It wasn't, clearly. The only thing that was important was the way his powerful hands held me, and the feel of his steely muscles. His midnight eyes boring into my very soul, taking me apart. One of his hands traced up my side, leaving a fiery trail in its wake. My entire world now was that hand on my ribs, caressing my bare skin.

When it skimmed over my breast, my back arched into him. My breath shallowed. But he hadn't told me how he felt yet. Was he going to admit his desire?

"Admit it, Galin. You still want me," I said. "Fate? It's bull-shit." Giddy, I laughed. My body hummed with need, but I forced myself to push him away again. He wasn't getting to touch me without giving me that one concession. But the way his shadowy magic licked at my skin, stroking my thighs, made my body heat.

When he refused to say a word, I pushed him away. There was some reason he couldn't tell me, but …

The cool night breeze caressed me, but I still felt hot. I crossed to the balcony that overlooked the pool. Pale moonlight glinted on the water.

Maybe the water of the pool could help me remember what I was supposed to be doing. The fairy wine was the problem, I thought.

I climbed up on the railing, and jumped.

I plunged under the water, and it felt divine against my naked skin. But I couldn't stop thinking about Galin, about the heat of his body, the feel of his hands on me. Blazing heat still filled me, and I wanted him in here with me.

When I came up for air, I saw that he'd joined me.

A wicked smile played about his lips as his gaze swept down my nearly naked body. Dark magic swirled round him, lashing the air.

"I think I drank too much of the fairy wine," I murmured.

He gave a slow shrug, moving toward me in the water. Why wasn't he speaking?

"What is it we're supposed to be—?"

But before I could finish, I felt his hand on my back. The tips of his fingers on my skin sent waves of pure pleasure radiating through me, and he made a quiet murmuring sound that trembled over me.

My pulse hammered out of control, molten desire racing through me as I stared into Galin's inscrutable gaze.

"Admit it out loud," I breathed. "We didn't need the mating bond."

In answer, he leaned down and crushed his lips against mine. My mouth opened, and our tongues swept together.

He pulled me tight to him, the grip of a man who'd never let me go.

As he kissed me hungrily, I knew only one thing for certain.

He'd been lying when he said he didn't want me anymore.

CHAPTER 34

GALIN

I pulled away from the kiss. Ali's eyes locked on mine, delirious with ecstasy.

Moonlight reflected in her silver irises. Her hair lay slick against her head; the lingerie Surtr had forced her to wear was nearly transparent.

That kiss—that carnal, animalistic kiss had awakened the bestial side in me. My fingers tightened on her waist, her hips. Elves were creatures of the earth, compelled to act on instinct. And all my instincts told me I needed to claim her.

She kept asking me to tell her that I desired her, because I'd stupidly tried to convince her, to convince myself that I felt nothing. She must be able to see now that it wasn't true.

I loved her, and it made no fucking sense without the mating bond. What was the point of the Norns if we felt this way without them? And yet here we were, clinging to each other in a silvery pool underneath the stars, when we should have been … doing something …

I couldn't remember what we should have been doing, because nothing existed in the nine realms right now but Ali.

Fairy wine. It was revealing our true feelings, and I

wanted to open my mouth and tell her it wasn't just the wine. That these emotions were real. But I couldn't make a fucking sound. I'd given my voice for something—was it for her? That would make sense. I'd give anything for her.

She ran a finger along the edge of my jaw, and a shudder rippled through every muscle in my body. I thought of tearing off the rest of her little clothing and sliding into her.

"Galin ..." Ali whispered. "I think this wine is very potent."

I drew her in, until her bare skin was pressed against mine. It wasn't just the wine for either of us, was it? I wanted to say it out loud. I wanted to explain, but I couldn't. I ached for her, to tell her everything. To have her.

Her eyes widened as I ran my hand along the curve of her back, feeling her soft skin.

"There was something about a sword," she whispered.

Even if I could have spoken, I wouldn't have been able to answer her with anything resembling coherent speech. All I could think about was the feel of her perfect body against me. I slid my hands all the way down under her ass, and lifted her. Her legs wrapped around my hips, and I pressed her against the edge of the pool. I had her right where I wanted her.

She nuzzled into me, her lips like burning embers along the side of my neck. Primal, dominating instincts tightened my muscles, and I thought of pulling aside her little panties, of biting her neck and thrusting into her ...

I had to restrain myself. There was a reason why, I thought ... More than one reason for restraint. There were so many reasons ...

It was just that after that kiss, the reasons escaped me.

I knew we were in the pool, but I couldn't feel the water any longer. Only Ali's soft skin under my fingers, the heat from her body wrapped around mine. I could feel her pulse, the rhythm of her heart beating against me.

Her hands slid down my chest, her expression mesmerized. An ancient instinct arced through me, hot as flames.

And then, my mind went blank. I lost any scrap of restraint I had, the chains on my resistance snapped. *She's mine.*

I leaned down, my lips crashing against her neck. I pressed my canines against her skin—just enough that she would know she was mine, rooting her in place with my hands, my teeth. Her thighs clenched around my body, back arching. She gasped loud, then moaned.

Ali and I belonged together. Fate or not, she was my mate, and I would claim her in the old way. My teeth pressed down harder. A groan escaped her, and her legs wrapped tighter around me. Her breasts, barely constrained by the camisole, pressed against my chest. My tongue swirled over where my teeth had been, tasting the faintest hint of blood.

I ran my fingers down her spine, thinking of ripping the lace off her. But before I could, I felt a new sensation: *her* teeth on my neck, piercing the skin. A low growl rose from her. It was as if I'd been struck by lightning. I couldn't speak, but my entire body shuddered with pleasure. She had an arm round the back of my head, and she pulled herself against me.

I ripped off the rest of her little camisole, exposing her perfect breasts completely, nipples peaked in the night air.

Oh gods. I couldn't think straight.

Her silver eyes were locked on mine. "You're wearing too many clothes Galin."

But she arched back, and I lowered my mouth to her breasts and took one of her nipples in my mouth. As my tongue teased her, her legs tightened like manacles.

But I wanted her totally and completely naked, stripped for me.

I reached down, ripping through the last bit of lacy fabric.

Mating bond or not, I'd give anything for this Night Elf. It made absolutely no sense.

And yet it was.

CHAPTER 35

ALI

A deep vibration, an insistent hum radiated from my core—a need that was both torture and pleasure at the same time. Just like the feel of his teeth at my throat.

Licking my lips, I forced myself to unlock my legs from him just long enough that I could help rip his trousers off. They were now the only barrier between me and satiation. I glanced down at the full length of him, my heart beating faster. I leaned back, resting my elbows over the edge of the pool. Once more, I wrapped my legs around him. A deep desire had built in me, and I needed to be filled. My thighs clenched around him.

His hand slid up my back, gripping my hair possessively, pulling my head back just a bit to expose my neck.

I shifted my hips, and I exhaled a shaky breath as he slid into me.

Pinning me to the side of the pool, he thrust hard, moving faster. His teeth were on my throat once more. An intense shiver ran through me, and the vibrating hum overtook my senses. My head fell back as I gasped, losing myself in waves of ecstasy. Galin gripped my waist roughly as he filled me again and again.

A moan escaped my lips and I threw my head back farther, staring at the stars that beamed above us. An intense and overwhelming pleasure was building inside me, and I brought down my gaze to look at Galin again. His eyes locked on mine.

As he plunged into me, I felt as if my soul were twining with his. The Norn had severed the soul bond; she had cut me free of him. Then why was I fucking him again, and why did it feel like love? Why did my heart feel like it was about to explode? Why was I calling his name over and over?

The water of the pool churned like a maelstrom. I clenched around him, body shattering. The pressure had passed the point of no return, and I felt my fingernails digging into his back. I was biting him again, because he was mine. My mind turned as black as his eyes, and my body went limp. I slumped against his chest, catching my breath.

Galin held me tight. My entire body felt like it was vibrating. Not like before—this was far softer, a sort of delicate, tingly feeling that came in soft waves.

Strangely, I realized tears were running down my cheeks, but I had no idea why. Galin stroked my hair.

"I'm sorry, I'm sorry," I kept saying. The fairy wine had made me delirious.

Galin scooped me up in his arms like I was a bride, and I looked up into his perfect face, a divine face. The darkness had faded from the whites of his eyes.

I brushed a lock of wet hair from his forehead. "Galin," I murmured. "There was something we were supposed to do."

My eyes started to close as he carried me. With my head nuzzled into him, he lifted me from the pool. I felt the water dripping off my naked body, and wondered if I should get some clothes.

There was a sword …

The bed was even softer than I remembered, and I found

myself sliding under the sheets. Galin slipped in behind me. His strong arms wrapped around me, pulling me close to him.

For the first time in years, I felt at peace.

If only I could remember what it was I was supposed to be doing.

CHAPTER 36

GALIN

I awoke cold and shivering. For a moment I panicked. Where was Ali? Then I felt her next to me, and I understood why I was freezing.

She had stolen the covers.

I reached over, trying to redistribute the blankets, but she only pulled them closer to herself.

"Mmmgghh …" she mumbled, still asleep. Then more clearly, "Nooo, Galin …"

But the room was ice cold, and I was naked. I tried again. This time as she pulled the covers away, I distinctly heard her call for Skalei. Now *that* was unnerving. She could potentially stab me in her sleep.

Even more unnerving, a shadow loomed at the edge of the bed.

I gripped the covers. Where was the sword? My chest unclenched only when I saw it lying on the floor. We really needed—

Galin, whispered a voice. My body went tense as I tried to make out who—or what—was talking to me.

Galin, said the voice again. *It is time to return to your queen.*

Dread slithered over my skin. The voice wasn't in the

room. It was in my own skull. There was, unfortunately, only one person I knew who could do that.

What are you doing here Ganglati? I answered in my thoughts.

You have broken your vow to the goddess. You were meant to be her consort. Not the Night Elf's. The shadow at the foot of the bed grew larger, lengthening until it loomed over me. Ganglati studied me with pale eyes.

Fuck.

My mind worked frantically. Was the shade really here at Hela's bidding? Or was something else going on? He and I weren't exactly friends. Even though he'd spent a week living within me, he'd been Hela's right-hand man for millennia.

I was going to have to choose my words carefully.

What are you talking about? A shiver rippled over my skin. The room was so cold now that my breath clouded each time I exhaled.

Ganglati's pale eyes shifted to where Ali slept next to me. He didn't have to speak for me to understand his meaning. *You cannot deny this.*

If they knew what Ali meant to me, her life would be in danger. I couldn't let them realize. *Oh, the Night Elf? She means nothing to me.*

That's not what our goddess thinks.

I frowned. He had to be lying. How could Hela know what I was thinking? She was trapped in Hel. I was in Vana-heim. Her power didn't extend beyond the walls of her realm.

Unless—I looked down at the runes and dark shadows swirling over my skin. A terrifying realization began to solidify in my brain.

She means nothing to me. I repeated the lie. *A bit of fun to pass the time. Nothing more.*

I see you found Surtr's sword, said Ganglati. *Did your Night Elf help you?*

What difference does it make? Panic was rising in me, and I cursed the fairy wine I'd been given. Ali needed the sword to fight the draugr. And Hela could use it to bring down the iron walls that surrounded her kingdom. Did Hela realize this?

You forget your master. The vapor that drifted off the runes on my chest began to thicken. Horror caught at me, as I understood that Hela's runes were more than just a loan of magic, more than a way to track me. They let the shade into my mind.

Worse, they let him control me. I felt my muscles stiffen as Ganglati took hold of me. *It is time you returned to your queen.*

I have lost my voice, I told him. *I cannot cast a spell.*

Do not worry about that.

If I couldn't fight the shade, Ali could. I was reaching for her to shake her awake, when my muscles locked. My arm stopped, my fingers clenched on air. I was stiff as a statue. Panic gripped me. I needed to be here to protect her. I needed her to have the sword, to stop the draugr.

You will do what I say, whispered the shade from the darkest recesses of my brain. *Now get the sword, and let's get out of here. The goddess needs it.*

My mind screamed, but I found myself doing as I was commanded, unable to resist.

The sword was in my hand, then I was vaguely aware that Ganglati was asking me to write something—a note to leave by Ali's side. I couldn't even focus on what I was writing. I was using all my mental energy to fight Ganglati's power. I raged against him, my soul screaming. For just a moment, I thought I'd broken free, that I could move my arm—

Then the shadowy magic on my chest began to condense.

Twisting around me like the coils of a serpent. Thicker and thicker, until my vision was completely obscured. A sharp tendril of horror coiled through me.

The chill deepened. My feet became ice, my fingers completely frozen. For a moment I was weightless. Drifting in a frigid void.

Then my feet were on solid ground again. And I heard a new voice—even more unwelcome in my ears.

"Welcome back, my king," said Hela. "I see you have completed my task. Now, let us go and free our people from the iron walls."

CHAPTER 37

ALI

I sat up in bed, instantly remembering what I'd been forgetting.

The sword. The fucking sword. The fairy wine had clouded my memory completely. I supposed I'd needed it to make the portal, but gods damn.

I needed that sword to defeat the draugr, and we had to—

I turned, looking at the empty space where Galin had been. And I could feel the icy chill of Hela's magic freezing the air. Almost as if she'd been here …

Inky magic spilled through the room, raising the hair on the back of my arms. It was like a residue of evil. Had Galin been using magic?

The sheets were still rumpled, and he'd pulled the covers off me. Where had he gone?

Whatever he was doing, I didn't have time to wait for his input. I crawled over to the edge of the bed to grab the sword—

My heart skipped a beat.

The sword was gone. With my head cleared, I was certain I'd left it there. The thing had been hot as coals, and I remembered pushing it off the bed onto the stone floor.

My pulse was hammering out of control, and I jumped out of bed. Had Galin done something with it?

I whirled, looking back at the bed. And now—I noticed something I hadn't seen before. A little note lying on the pillow.

With a thundering heart, I crossed to pick it up.

I am bringing the sword to my goddess and queen, Hela. Do not try to come for me, or Barthol will be slaughtered.

    -Galin

It was his handwriting. I'd know it anywhere.

Betrayal cut me open, sharp as a knife in my heart. He was still loyal to her.

I drew in a breath, waiting for the rage and burning anger that was sure to come, but to my surprise it was sadness that clenched at my heart. A lead weight of despair dragged me down to the bed.

Be angry, I told myself.

But my body was shaking uncontrollably, and all I could think was that he'd betrayed me. Why would he do that?

Maybe he really didn't feel anything for me. Perhaps—in the pool—that had just been the fairy wine. And now that the effects had worn off …

Angry now, I wiped a few tears away with the back of my hand.

I'd severed the bond between us. Last night had been a lie. He felt nothing.

A few deep breaths, clenching my jaw.

Galin or not—I still had to find a way to save this kingdom. I still had to get that sword back.

Cold fury rippled through me as I pulled open a drawer and grabbed some clothes to slip into—black pants and a shirt. I crossed into the living room, startled to see the sun was already starting to rise, tinging the sky with peach.

"Ali?" said a muffled voice through the door.

"Yes?" I pulled it open to see Swegde. I stared, unable to come up with the words to tell him I'd failed.

"I heard you screaming for Galin."

My throat was tight. "I have some bad news. We talked to the giants in Muspelheim. We were able to get the sword."

"Why is that bad news?"

My jaw clenched. "Galin seems to have stolen it to give to Hela."

Swegde went completely pale. "How can you be sure? He seemed to genuinely want to help. I can usually tell when someone is mendacious."

For a moment, doubt flickered. But, no. "He left a note."

He shook his head. "Could it be ambiguous? Maybe a miscommunication."

"It says *I am bringing the sword to my goddess and queen, Hela.* And he signed his name. Oh, and he will kill my brother if I come for it." Icy anger laced my tone.

"What are you going to do?" asked Swegde.

Pain seared me. I didn't want to sacrifice Barthol—but I simply had no other choice than to try to get out of Hel with both my brother and the sword. "I'll go after him. How much longer can you keep the draugr at bay?"

"One more day, maybe—" Swegde looked down. "It's really bad. Yesterday some broke through the walls. They climb over each other. They turned my men—it's hard to hurt the ones you love even when they're so freshly dead."

"I'll get the sword back. I promise." I said it with more confidence than I felt.

I whirled, scribing the portal spell, thinking of my love for Barthol. How I'd bring him back—despite what Galin had said. The portal opened in a flash, blazing brightly and filling the room with a crackling static.

"Oh wow," breathed Swegde. "You've gotten really good."

Right now my people needed me. And when I found Galin, there would be Hel to pay.

CHAPTER 38

ALI

I stepped through the portal and into the depths of Hel. My feet squelched in black mud, cold rain spattered my shirt. This time, the cold didn't bother me. Behind me, the portal shut with a sizzling pop.

I'd managed to conjure the portal in the right place this time. Just in front of me was the narrow crack Barthol and I had snuck through. I glanced left and right, double checking there were no shades watching me. Then, quickly, I dropped down and crawled inside.

I moved as fast as I could through the air shaft, passing over Hela's chambers and making my way straight to the throne room. Breathing hard, I scanned the vast hall.

Shades darkened the ancient flagstones. Row upon row of them stood or hovered like solemn statues, right up to the edge of Hela's throne. The hall was deathly silent, like all of Hel was holding its breath.

At last, I saw Hela, dressed in a white gossamer gown, her eyes gleaming with excitement. Galin lounged in a throne a few feet away. His eyes were downcast, his jaw rigid. Black vapor streamed off his skin. He was ready to do something terrible, I was certain of it.

Anger flared in my heart, swirling with confusion. Why allow me to come along with him if he'd planned to betray me all along? Had he known he might need someone else who could conduct magic, that he could lose his voice?

I forced myself to tear my gaze away, only to see something even worse. Barthol stood in the shadows just next to Hela's throne. Dressed in his favorite cave bear jacket, he looked even bigger than I remembered. His eyes were fixed on Hela, but instead of a look of resolute anger, all I could see was an expression of blissful rapture spread across his face. I wanted to throw up.

Hela spoke then, her voice a sharp hiss over the crowd. "Are we ready?"

Below me, the shades cheered—a terrifying sound like a thousand cave bears sharpening their claws. The hair on the back of my neck rose with fear.

"Now," said Hela, "I am going to free *my* people."

And this was why Galin had brought her Surtr's sword. She picked it up from the floor. As she raised it above her head, flames began to lick along the blade.

"I have the sword of the fire giants," she shouted. "I will use it to carve through the iron wall. I will create a new gate. Not an entrance, but an exit from this vile place. We will travel into the realms of the living."

The shades cheered again.

"I will rule each of the nine worlds, a goddess among the dead! We will be free!"

Then, holding the sword above her head like a talisman, she jumped down from her throne. Around her swarmed the shades in a vortex of spectral darkness. At her heels strode Galin and Barthol.

An idea began to take root, as it became clear that she had total control over both of them.

Maybe this hadn't been Galin's choice. What did I

believe? Did I believe that he truly loved me—without the mating bond? Without the fairy wine?

The thoughts twisted wildly in my mind. The only thing I knew for sure was that Hela was my enemy. And she would not be easy to take down.

I watched as they walked, a grim procession.

I thought at first that they were going to cross out through the main passage. But partway across the room, Hela stopped and turned to face the wall.

Lowering Surtr's sword to her side, she raised her free hand. Her fingers twitched like the legs of a dying insect as she scribed a rapid series of runes. In front of her the stones of the wall began to shiver and tremble, then with a sharp report, they cracked open, revealing a new passage. Immediately she strode inside with Barthol, Galin, and the shades piling in behind.

I watched all this holding my breath. When the last shade crossed into the passage, I saw the rocks begin to shimmer.

And that was my cue to leap out from my hiding spot, to sprint across the broken flagstones. I slipped into the passage just as the door closed behind me with a resounding thunk.

* * *

SHADOWS FILLED THE TUNNEL, and dark alcoves and crevices. That meant I could move behind Hela's party undetected.

I hurried along behind them, slipping between shadowy nooks for what seemed like hours. Finally, the passage sloped upwards. A cold breeze brought with it the wet scent of decay.

We were close to the muddy plains of Hel.

Hela and the shades slipped out of the tunnel through a wide opening. I crept up as close as I dared, and peered out.

The tunnel opened onto a low hillside—muddy and wet, with misting rain filling the air.

A hundred yards off, I saw the dark shape of the iron wall of Hel. Dripping with a rusty trickle of water, it looked just as cold and unpleasant as I remembered.

At the base of the wall stood the goddess, my brother, and Galin. And around them, thousands of shades, each transfixed by their queen.

A light blazed in the semi-darkness. Hela had raised Surtr's sword above her head again, and it cast warm light in the gloom, burning with a preternatural fire. She was shouting, but I was too far away to hear the words distinctly. The sword blazed brighter, and she turned to face the wall.

She was about to carve through it, and somehow I had to stop her.

"Skalei."

A dagger. That was all I had. As the blade appeared in my hand, I leapt up and hurled it at the goddess. It arced through the air, slicing through the drizzle like an arrow. Just like Swegde had taught me. A wet thunk sounded across the muddy field as it struck the goddess in the back.

Hela shrieked, dropping the sword. She staggered, clutching for the hilt that now protruded between her shoulder blades.

I didn't stay to watch. Instead I raced down the hillside, my eyes fixed on Surtr's sword where it lay steaming in the mud.

As Hela screamed, pandemonium reigned. The shades flew about like angry bees unsure who'd disturbed their hive. My brother stood only a few feet from the goddess, his mouth half open.

I'd have asked him to help, but clearly he would not.

I dodged between shades, closing the gap. Thirty, twenty, ten, I was five feet from the blade, when a heavy body slammed into my side, throwing me to the mud. I tried to scramble up, but a massive hand held me down in the muck.

Galin stared at me, eyes dark as night. He pinned me down, holding me in an iron grip, one hand on each of my wrists, a knee on my stomach.

I stared up at him. Did I believe that he loved me, despite everything? Despite taking the sword, the note he'd left, despite the fact that he appeared to be thwarting my attempts down here?

When I looked into his eyes, I felt it again. Our souls twining. Underneath it all—yes, I did think he loved me.

This was Hela's work.

And even if I had to try to kick the shit out of him right now, I would save him from her too.

Out of the corner of my eye I saw Surtr's sword, only a few feet away. So close.

I headbutted Galin, smashing my forehead into his nose, but his grip didn't let up. Snarling, I brought my knee up into his crotch—for which I would apologize when I got him out of here. At last, I was able to shove him off me, and I scrambled up. Now there was nothing left except the sword…

She was there in a flash. Hela stood over me, holding Skalei to my throat. Pure rage contorted her otherwise beautiful face, and a thin trickle of blood ran from the side of her mouth to her chin.

She twirled the blade. "Is this yours?"

I tried to call for it, but all that came out of my mouth was a guttural grunting sound. Hela had taken control of my tongue.

She held Skalei above my head. "This is a very nice dagger."

I waited for her to slash downwards, to kill me and be done with it, but instead she turned the blade over in her hands. "I haven't seen a blade like this in a thousand years. Very rare. Very valuable."

I wanted to scream at her, to call Skalei to me, but my tongue wouldn't move.

"Very valuable. Which is why it's so unfortunate that I have to destroy it."

Pure panic rolled over me as Hela adjusted her grip on Skalei. Her shadow magic slipped over it, twisting the blade beyond recognition. It flexed, then shattered with a sharp crack.

But I hardly noticed, because a white-hot pain lanced down my arm as the silver tattoos that bound Skalei to me blazed with magic.

A storm of pain engulfed my mind.

CHAPTER 39

GALIN

I felt as shattered as Ali's blade. Desperately, I wanted to get her out of here, but sharp vines of icy magic spread through my body, keeping me under Hela's control.

With Ali vanquished, Hela seemed to grow in strength. Blood dripped from her lips, and a rapturous smile spread across her face. Her pearlescent skin was practically glowing, and her indigo tattoos grew more bright. The Goddess of the Dead was ready to become the Goddess of the Nine Worlds. She'd rule both sun and rain, darkness and light, life and death. With only a sea of the draugr around her.

In moments she would use Surtr's sword to carve her way out of Hel. Free from the iron walls, she'd rule the nine realms as the only living god.

There would be no check on this Hela; she would never be controlled, never vanquished.

"King Galin, it is time you joined me at my side." Her voice was a ringing bell in my mind, one I could not ignore.

The goddess knelt to pick up the sword. This time when she raised it, she didn't brandish it above her head for the adulation of the shades. She simply leveled the blade at the iron wall. Surtr's sword began to glow, brighter and brighter. Hela became a silhouette, a wavering shadow behind incandescent light, then the blade blazed so brightly I couldn't see her at all.

Hela's magic encased my mind like a gate of darkness, iron walls within my skull.

When I'd been trapped before, I'd used portals. Love was the way to travel through walls, to transport to another place. I thought of Ali's eyes as she looked up at me, the feeling of my soul entwining with hers—even if it wasn't meant to be.

Love warmed me from within, melting the ice of Hela's magic.

I could move again, move my hands …

I started to run for Hela, but a blast of hot magic knocked me back again. A tremendous report rent the air, the tearing of ancient magic. Then, the air filled with primal screams of joy as the shades realized what had happened. The light of the sword faded.

My heart was ready to wither in my chest. I'd meant to free her—but only after we'd trapped the draugr. This was a disaster.

A vast crack marred the iron wall. Hela stood beaming, molten metal glowing at her feet, as hundreds and hundreds of shades streamed past and into the nine worlds.

Why? I wanted to scream at her. *Why did you do this?*

But I couldn't speak. My throat was as dry, as parched, as broken as always.

So I could only watch when she walked towards me, hands raised. I could not kill a goddess—not without Loki's wand, not without my voice.

"I have freed my people. There is nothing here for me," her voice rasped. "It is bleak. It is dark. It is full of souls, but it has no *life*. The gods are dead. It is only right that a goddess should rule the nine worlds. The elves will die. The giants, too. Some now, some tomorrow. But other things will live. That's the brilliance of my plan. When their corporeal bodies perish, they won't have to live in Hel. They can stay exactly where they fell. In Midgard, Vanaheim—don't you see? I am saving the world."

Every kingdom will become a kingdom of death! I screamed in my mind.

Hela beamed. "It is time that I reacquainted my shades with their bodies. They should not be left mouldering in the dirt."

She plucked Levateinn from her belt, and turned again to face the jagged hole in the wall.

CHAPTER 40

ALI

The heat from Surtr's sword had been so intense that my only option had been to press myself into the mud, cover my head with my hands, and hope I wasn't burnt to a crisp.

The good news was that I was unharmed. The bad news was that the heat of the blade had hardened Hel's black mud into a brick-like crust. Now I was trapped, stuck like a bug in flypaper, barely able to breathe, and not able to see anything other than the grime and dirt in front of my face.

This was disastrous, and panic slid through my veins. Hela would destroy the nine realms.

Strong hands grabbed me under the shoulders and tore me free. Even as I gulped down air, terrible pain twisted around my wrists and forearms. The severed runes of Skalei's binding spell burned with preternatural fire, and a deep agony filled my heart as I thought of what Hela had done to my blade.

I might have given up then, but I saw Galin's face. His eyes shone even in the darkness of Hel, the mesmerized look gone. He was back.

I knew then that I'd been right—even if he couldn't speak to say what he felt, I could see it in his eyes.

He took one of my hands and pressed it to his bare chest. As the shadowy vapors circled my fingers, I felt his warm skin, his heart beating, thrumming within him.

My eyes widened. There was more than that churning under the surface: I could feel his emotions, his feelings, his desires. He continued to look at me, his eyes demanding my attention.

He pointed at Hela. She'd turned from us again, and I saw silver shimmering in the darkness. She held Levateinn, Loki's wand. Whatever she was going to do with it, it couldn't be good. I stared, watching the shades pour through the hole in the wall. There was no sign of Barthol.

Then, Galin pointed at the dried mud, where he'd scratched a symbol, roughly the shape of a circle. And next to it, a word: Asgard. His eyes fixed on mine as he pressed my hand harder against his chest. I could feel his heart, deep and strong, booming like a cannon behind his ribs.

He wasn't scared. He wasn't calm either. He was steadfast, brave, and filled with love.

We were supposed to portal to Asgard. I didn't know why, or what the plan was.

I only knew that I trusted him more than anything.

He pulled me in close. My heart might have been beating wildly, but as I began to scribe a portal rune I felt completely, utterly safe.

CHAPTER 41

GALIN

I allowed my emotions to pour into Ali, strengthening and fortifying her magic. As our powers mixed, relief flooded me, and a sense of peace. Somehow I knew that whatever happened next, it'd be okay.

Out of the corner of my eye, I saw Hela scribing the final runes—the ones that brought back life. It was the very spell I'd used to bring her back from the dead. In a moment, she'd reanimate all the shades that had just entered Vanaheim and Midgard. Thousands of living corpses, each one a draugr ready to feed on any living human or elf that remained.

But I would stop her. Odin had shown me the way in Mimisbrunnr.

Hela was almost finished, only a few runes left before the spell would be complete. Likewise, I sensed that Ali was full of our magic, her spell ready—just a single rune remained. Timing would be crucial.

Hela's wand twitched—three, two, one. She scribed the last rune. A momentary pause.

I grabbed Ali's hand.

Shimmering magic sprang from Hela's wand, a silver streak, racing towards the hole in the wall.

Now! I jerked Ali's arm down. Together we completed the final rune. An electric pop crackled in the air, and a massive portal filled the hole in the wall. Hela's spell slammed into it — then passed through.

Into Asgard.

The air shimmered for a second, then the portal vanished. For a long moment, nothing moved but the falling rain. Ali leaned against me, spent from the magic.

Hela's voice was like a curse in my mind. *What have you done?*

She spun towards Ali and me. There was no sign of the wand, only Surtr's sword blazing in her grasp. I threw Ali out of the goddess's path, then shadow jumped towards Hela.

I was unarmed, and going up against an immortal goddess. There was no way I could win. But I didn't need to win. I just needed to stall her.

The sword's fire blazed towards me. Hela's voice cut like a knife. "You cannot defeat me."

I ignored her, shadow jumping to her side. Before she could swing the blade, I punched her as hard as I could in the side of the head.

As she staggered, I grabbed for the sword. But already, she'd regained her footing. She threw me down, the force impossibly powerful. I slammed backward into the caked mud.

In the next moment, her foot was on my throat, pressing down. She pointed the sword at Ali.

"Now watch as you lose everything," she murmured.

The sword began to glow. Ali tried to run, but she was far too slow. I summoned the dark magic that filled my body, then shadow jumped again. I smashed into Ali, throwing her out of the path of the arc of fire. I leapt up again and whirled to face the goddess.

Hela stalked towards us. "I seem to have discovered your

weakness, King Galin," she hissed. "Do you want to die first, or second?" She raised the sword, and fire licked along the blade.

But a distant tremor, like the aftershock of an earthquake, shook the hardened mud under my feet.

Hela stiffened, her eyes suddenly widening. Her expression was no longer triumphant. "What have you done?" She stalked towards me, pointing the flaming sword at my chest.

Then, her gaze dipped to the word I'd written in the dried mud. *Asgard.*

"No …" she snarled.

Electricity flashed, and a portal snapped open. Instantly, a silver lightning bolt shot through the air, striking Hela in the center of the chest.

A god dressed in chainmail strode through the portal, his body glowing. He gripped an enormous hammer.

"What in Odin's name is going on here?" he bellowed, and his voice rumbled over the landscape.

Hela's dress was now singed, smoke rising from it. "Thor." She spat his name like a curse.

As I heard his name, joy rippled through me. Odin's plan had worked. With Ali's help, we'd sent Hela's spell into Asgard. Instead of reviving elves and humans, she'd breathed new life into dead gods.

Even as I felt profound relief, pandemonium erupted around us. More and more portals appeared. Enormous men and women entered Hel.

The beautiful Freyja with golden hair, Tyr with his missing arm. A lithe hooded god—Loki. Odin, with his single sapphire eye.

The gods and goddess gathered round us, towering over Hela.

Odin's gaze swung to Ali and me. I saw now the full planes of his face, wrinkled and lined, the black eye patch covering his missing eye. The cost of a knowledge we both now bore. "Who are these two?" Then, his single eye narrowed. "You are the ones who freed us?"

Ali stood, dusting herself off. "I'm Ali, Empress of the Elves. I made a portal into Asgard, so Hela's magic would raise you." She glanced at me. "This is Galin, the world's greatest sorcerer."

Odin frowned. "He can't speak for himself?"

Ali cleared her throat. "He traded his voice—his magic—for knowledge in Mimisbrunnr's water."

"Ahhh …" Odin's eye gleamed as he took me in. "Of course. I remember."

I stared in wonder as Thor escorted Hela away, and the gods began the work of bringing the world alive once more.

Once, I'd believed nothing was more important than the gods, than fate. That reversing Ragnarok was more important than anything—bringing the world alive again. Raising the gods from their sleep. Now, I'd send them all back to the grave to keep Ali safe.

I'd live in a frozen Hel if it meant she was keeping my bed warm at night.

CHAPTER 42

ALI

Galin and I drove along the banks of the Charles River. He'd found a thousand-year-old car rotting in a parking garage, and we'd healed the thing using magic.

Now, as I looked at the sun sparkling on the water, I was reminded again of how much had changed in Boston and Cambridge since the gods' return. The snow had melted, the cold wind had been replaced by warm sun. In places green grass was growing.

Odin had lifted the curse that created the draugr. They'd all become alive again. Suddenly, Cambridge was teeming with young humans. I'd been helping Galin and the High Elves get them fed and housed, which was actually pretty fun.

"Hello? Testing. Testing," a voice boomed from part of the car. It took me a moment to realize it was the radio. "Testing. Testing. One. Two. Three." A pause followed, then a man said, "Guys I think this is actually working."

"Galin," I said, "this must be one of the humans brought to life again. They are fascinating, aren't they? And they're getting all this old technology functioning again."

Before I could continue, the most glorious music filled the car. It was a song I'd never heard before, and I listened transfixed until it was finished.

I waited for another song to play, but the voice was talking now about how amazing it was to be back now that Ragnarok was over. Galin poked a knob and the voice quieted.

I turned to him, my heart full of excitement, and he pulled over so we could have a view of the dazzling sun setting over the river. He leaned back in his seat, and the look he was giving me suggested he wanted to do filthy things with me.

"That song was great. Did you hear the lyrics? All about not getting pushed around. If you fail, if you falter, you get back to your feet. Galin, it was like what happened to us. I truly thought you'd abandoned me. When I woke up and saw the note, written in your handwriting. I thought you were gone. I thought without the mating bond, you felt nothing. I'd never been that down before. But do you know what? I didn't give up." Tears filled my eyes. "I saw you, and I knew I shouldn't give up hope. If life crushes you, you have to fight." I wiped a tear away. "That's what that song means. You keep going."

Galin nodded, an amused smile on his face. I had the faint sense that he thought I was ridiculous, but that he loved me too.

"Do you know what the song is? The name of it?"

His expression grew resigned. He picked up his notebook and wrote in it, then handed it to me.

I frowned. The name made no sense. "Are you sure this is right?"

Galin nodded vigorously, his lips still curled in a smile.

I shook my head in disbelief. Humans from a thousand years ago were really strange.

"Do you have this song in your record collection?"

His face looked pained, like I'd just told him I wanted him to try my pickle and mayonnaise salad. But, slowly he nodded.

"Yes!" I grinned. I was definitely going to listen to "Tubthumping" by Chumbawamba a whole bunch more when we got home.

The sun dipped lower in the sky. I wanted to stay in Midgard forever, but I had to return to Vanaheim soon, too.

Whenever I returned, Swegde was there waiting for me, with news about cattle and crops.

Galin wrote in his notebook. *How is Barthol doing?*

I frowned. "Surprisingly fine, considering what he went through. He's opening a nightclub in Midgard called To Hel and Back." I sighed. "Galin? Do you miss having your voice?"

He shook his head. Then, he wrote in his notebook. I peered over his shoulder as he wrote.

From the first day we met in the Citadel's dungeon, to when you saved me from the Nokk—because and in spite of your terrible taste in music—I've been yours. The mating bond does not matter, fate does not matter. My voice and my magic do not matter. We belong to each other.

And I was not whole until I met you.

When we raised the gods, when you pressed your hand to my chest and channeled my love into your heart, I felt more perfectly whole than I'd ever felt. Love filled me, and that was because of you.

Fortunately, I do not need a voice to make you shudder with pleasure and claw your fingernails down my back. I don't need a voice when I can make you scream my name over and over. And I plan to spend the rest of my days doing just that.

My eyes went misty, and I smiled at him. I'd be saving that piece of paper.

Galin, like all great warriors, knew that when life kicked the shit out of him, you didn't give up. And that was why we belonged together.

EPILOGUE

SWEGDE

I stepped out of the portal into Valhalla, not sure what to expect. Ali had told me that the valkyries were wild, but the sheer quantity of filth and destruction was unlike anything I'd ever seen.

In the middle of a great marble hall they'd scratched out a fire pit. In one corner hung the gutted bodies of four stags, while next to the fire was a giant oak cask; this must be the mead that Ali had told me about.

Around the borders of the hall, through arches, servants bustled around, cleaning, ferrying food to the gods. Most of the hall gleamed with gold and burnished marble, the sun rays lighting up the room. It seemed that Hela's magic had revived not only the gods in Valhalla, but every living servant as well.

Only, none of them came near the valkyries' area, and it was the one patch of filth within the realm. The servants, I imagined, were terrified of the valkyries.

Feeling lost, I sat down on a tree stump someone had left by the fire pit.

For a thousand years, little in my life had changed—until Ali showed up. Then, I was teaching an Empress how to throw a blade, the names of the trees in the great forest. Helping her learn how to rule.

Seeing Vanaheim through her eyes had stirred something within me that had been dormant for years.

Not love, but something like it—the feeling of being close to someone. But with Galin taking a permanent place at her side, we wouldn't be as close anymore.

I still had plenty to do. I'd been sent to collect the horses Galin and Ali had ridden across the desert. After that, I was the one to tell Harald and Sigre that Galin was now King of Midgard. Then I was the one to arrest them when they tried to murder me.

I'd even tried to organize homes for all of those brought to life again. That was, perhaps, the hardest thing I'd ever done, and everyone had complaints.

And now, I had a delivery for the valkyries. And I had no idea what to expect.

I rose again, surveying the hall of the gods. What was I supposed to do here? "Hello?" I called out, gripping Gjallarhorn. "Anyone here? I have a drinking horn to return to the valkyries." I couldn't exactly just leave it on the tree stump. It was far too valuable.

No one responded. Were the valkyries out for a ride?

I stared at the detritus strewn around the fire pit. Drinking horns, gnawed bones. Then I heard the sound of feminine voices.

"Gondul." The voice echoed off the walls. "Can I play with Mimi? He's such a good listener."

"No!" came the sharp reply. "You know he's been confiscated."

"Awww …"

Then I saw them. Six statuesque women, with long braids that cascaded over their armor. True warriors.

I cleared my throat, gripping the drinking horn. "Hello."

The valkyries stopped and stared.

At last the largest one said, "Who are you?"

"I'm Swegde."

"I'm Gondul—"

"And I'm Hildr," said the valkyrie standing just next to her.

"What are you doing in our home?" asked Gondul.

"Empress Ali asked me to return this." I lifted the horn.

But Gondul didn't seem interested in Gjallarhorn. "What is that outfit you're wearing?"

Confused, I looked down at my clothes. I was wearing a leather vest and buckskin pants. My usual clothing. "Is there something wrong?"

The big valkyrie's brow furrowed. "Where are the sleeves?"

I don't know what came over me at that moment, but I found myself flexing my muscles, a smile on my lips. "Sleeves get in the way when I wrestle with bears."

The valkyrie's mouth dropped open. "You wrestle with bears?"

I did once. "All the time."

The valkyrie quirked her eyebrow. "So you like to fight? You are a warrior?"

I wasn't sure whether to be intimidated or not, but I sensed that these women didn't appreciate weakness. "I am, truly, a warrior."

"You hear that, ladies?" Gondul raised her hands to the ceiling. "This one *likes* to fight."

Oh gods. What had I gotten myself into?

Gondul stepped forward, a wicked grin on her face. "Wanna fight and wrestle with us?"

I blinked, unable to come up with a reasonable response. At last, I said, "I guess so."

The valkyries cheered excitedly, swarming round me.

They smelled of sweat and stale mead, but I didn't mind. These were women of the earth, fighters like me. Gondul slapped me on the shoulder. "We wrestle first, then we fight. Then we drink."

I found my eyes fixed on the big valkyrie. She was, I decided, one of the most beautiful women I'd ever met. Strong callused fingers. Thick ropes of braids. And she wanted to wrestle with me?

She began to peel off her armor. I wasn't sure why, but I was transfixed by her skin—smooth and unscarred. She kept her eyes locked on mine. Blue as the sea.

"Should I …" I cleared my throat. "Undress?"

She shook her head. "No, keep your clothes on."

"But it'll give me an advantage."

"Don't worry about an advantage." The valkyrie stalked towards me, and I glanced at the others. I'd been so focused on Gondul, I hadn't noticed that they'd also stripped down. Six athletic, half-naked women stared at me hungrily. Instinct kicked in, and I stepped back.

"You see," said Gondul, "it's six to one."

Then, shouting to the other valkyries, she leapt into the air.

As the valkyries threw themselves on me, I couldn't help but think of Ali.

This was why she had sent *me* to return Gjallarhorn.

Thank you, I thought. *Thank you so very much.*

THE FALLEN

SAMPLE CHAPTER

When I was a kid, I dreamt of living in the castle that loomed over our city, a place of magic and intrigue. As I got older, I started to learn that even the slums had their own kind of magic. If you knew where to look, you could feel the power of ancient kings thrumming under the stones beneath your feet.

Tonight, warm lights shone through some of the windows through the fog, and the sound of a distant piano floated on the wind, winding between narrow alleys. No one was out here, just me and the salty breeze, the shadows growing longer as the sun slid lower in the sky. The mist curled around brick tenements that groaned toward each other, crooked with age. Fog skimmed over the dark, cobbled street.

I didn't care what anyone thought—this city was beautiful.

I shoved my hands in my pockets, glad the day was over. Like every Friday night, I was heading for the Bibliotek Music Hall. Some lovely chap would buy me a drink. I'd dance till the sun came up and the blackbirds started to sing.

I knew every alley, every hiding spot, every haunted corner where pirates once hung in gallows. I'd grown up to the sound of the seagulls overhead and the lapping of the Dark River against the embankment.

But tonight as I walked, the sense of wonder started to darken a little. The shadows seemed to thicken.

Every now and then, the crowded streets could feel like a trap. Because as much as I loved the place, it wasn't necessarily populated by gentlemen.

And right now, the familiar magic was being replaced by a sense of menace. It lingered in the air, making goosebumps rise on my skin, but I wasn't sure why.

I picked up my pace, envisioning the fresh bread and cheese I'd get at the Bibliotek Music Hall. Maybe I just needed a proper snack.

But why did I feel like someone was following me?

When I sniffed, I smelled whale oil, pitch pine and turpentine. Ah. Bloody hell. That was what had me on edge. The Rough Boys—a gang who lived on an old boat in the docks—always reeked of their ship. I could smell them from here, even if I couldn't see them yet.

Were they following me? Had I stolen something that belonged to them? I spent my days on the docks, in and out of ships and warehouses. I pilfered tea and other valuables, passing them off to a network of thieves.

Not glamorous, admittedly, but it was honest work.

Okay, fine. It wasn't honest either, but it meant I got to eat.

I glanced over my shoulder, and that was when my pulse kicked up a notch. I swallowed hard. Three of them stood at the end of the street, fog billowing around them like ghost ships on a misty sea. I recognized them right away by their signature look—shaggy hair and pea coats.

"Oi! Pussycat!" One of them shouted for me, voice

booming off stone walls. "I got a message for your mum! She needs to pay up."

"No thanks!" I shouted.

I knew how they sent messages—with their blades, carved in skin. Mum owed them money, which meant I owed them money. And if I didn't pay up they'd take a knife to me fast.

I whirled and raced through the narrow street.

"It's not exactly optional!" One of them shouted after me.

Where were the bloody coppers when you needed them? Always around when I pinched something, but never when cutthroats were after me.

At least I knew these streets as well as I knew my own body. If I could keep up the pace, I could lose the bastards.

My feet hammered the pavement, arms pumping as I ran. My brown curls streamed behind me. Puddles soaked into my socks through the holes in my threadbare shoes. I wanted to look behind me, to see how close they were, but that little movement would cost me. I knew if I slowed down, there'd be more of their gang crawling from the shadows. Fear was giving me speed.

The Rough Boys took people's noses, eyelids, ears. If I could avoid it, I'd prefer not to walk around like a mutilated horror show for the rest of my life.

So as they chased me, I dodged from one dark alley to the next, rounding the labyrinthine corners, keeping to the shadows, trying to lose them.

But the Rough Boys were taller than me, and just as fast, sprinting like jackals over the stones.

"Lila, is it? Pretty lady." One of them shouted. "We just need to have a little chat."

Did they think if they called me pretty I'd simper over to them, blushing?

I was good in a fight—better than most men, even—but a

fight with a gang in their territory was always a losing prospect. There were always more of them ready to slink out of alleys. My sister Alice taught me never to draw your knife unless you knew you could win.

Except I couldn't run forever, and I needed just a moment to catch my breath. At twenty-five, I was already getting slow. Embarrassing.

Breathless, I took a sharp turn onto Dagger Row. Then I darted into a shadowy alley between two brick walls. I hid deep in the darkness, listening with relief as the cutthroats ran on past. Oblivious.

A smile curled my lips. *You lived another night.*

Perhaps I'd make it to twenty-six with my face intact.

For just a moment, I rested, hands on my thighs. Crowded tenements rose up on either side of me. Dirty water ran in the gutters. I straightened again and peered out from the alley.

No one around.

I pulled the hood of my coat tight, then started walking at a fast clip.

The winding streets had taken me on a jagged path back toward the river. Before I crossed onto the next street, I peered around the corner to the right. I shivered at the sight of Castle Hades.

The ancient fortress was still breathtaking, every time I looked at it. Its dark stone loomed over a bustling city of merchants and beggars, holy sisters and street crawlers. We all looked up to it with awe.

The castle's four central towers rose up like ancient obelisks against the night sky. Two enormous rings of stone walls fortified the exterior, and a moat surrounded it. Once, the castle had gleamed white in the sun, and lions roamed the courtyards. Just fifty years ago, ravens had swooped over its twenty-one towers, and true Albian kings and queens danced in the courtyards.

Back then, we used to think the ravens protected Dovren. That they were good luck.

But the ravens had done nothing when invaders arrived on the Dark River—an army of elite warriors, headed by the ruthless Count Saklas. The ravens didn't help at all when Count Saklas beheaded our king in his own dungeon.

Now, the count ruled the whole kingdom from the castle's stone walls. Our citizens hung from gallows and gibbets outside, macabre warnings. Anyone who opposed his rule got the death penalty.

Pretty sure the bastard killed the ravens, too, because of course he did.

Two years ago, the last time anyone saw my sister Alice, she was carrying red silks into the castle. Then, she just disappeared. No idea what happened to her. It felt like the castle had swallowed her up.

Shivering, I turned away, thinking warmly of the Bibliotek Music Hall. My friend Zahra would be waiting for me, probably already with a cocktail in hand. In my pocket, I had a tiny nip of whiskey, and I pulled it out to take a sip and warm myself up. Cheap and strong, it burned my throat.

Maybe the count had conquered my country, but we still had the best music in the world. And we knew how to throw a party.

But just as I was starting to let down my guard, the sound of footfalls echoed behind me. I whirled, and fear jolted me as dark shadows emerged from the fog.

Bloody hell. The Rough Boys had found me again.

The Fallen is available in ebook and print over on
Amazon.com

For a full list of our books, check out our website.

https://www.cncrawford.com/books/

And a possible reading order.

https://www.cncrawford.com/faq/

ACKNOWLEDGMENTS

Thanks especially to Christine all her suggestions and assistance. Our editor and proofreader Jen was awesome editing and polishing this book into a something I'm proud to publish. Carlos made us a particularly beautiful cover. And, last but not least, thanks so much to our advanced reader team for their help, and to C.N. Crawford's Coven on Facebook!